Maigret Afraid

Maigret Afraid

GEORGES SIMENON

**Translated from the French
by MARGARET DUFF**

A Harvest Book
A Helen and Kurt Wolff Book
Harcourt Brace and Company
San Diego New York London

Requests for permission to make copies
of any part of the work should be mailed to:
Permissions Department, Harcourt Brace & Company,
6277 Sea Harbor Drive, Orlando, Florida 32887-6777.

Maigret is a registered trademark of the Estate of
Georges Simenon.

Library of Congress Cataloging-in-Publication Data
Simenon, Georges, 1903–1989
Maigret afraid.
Translation of Maigret a peur.
"A Helen and Kurt Wolff book."
I.   Title.
PQ2637.I53M255113   1983   843′.912   82-23233
ISBN 0-15-655142-X (Harvest pbk.)

The text was set in Times Roman.

Printed in the United States of America
First Harvest edition 1984
H G F E D

Maigret Afraid

1

Quite suddenly, between two small stations, whose names he could not make out, and of which he saw hardly anything in the darkness, except the driving rain against a large lamp and figures of men pushing wagons, Maigret wondered what he was doing there.

Perhaps he had dozed off for a moment in the overheated compartment? He could not have lost consciousness completely, because he knew he was in a train; he could hear its monotonous noise; he would have sworn that he had continually seen, every so often in the dark expanse of fields, the lighted windows of an isolated farm. All this, and the smell of soot mingling with that of his damp clothes, remained real, and also a steady murmur of voices in a nearby compartment, but it was in some way not entirely real; it was no longer very clearly situated in space, let alone in time.

He might have been somewhere else, in any little train traveling through the countryside, and he himself might have been a fifteen-year-old Maigret returning from school on a Saturday on a local train exactly like this one, with ancient cars, their couplings creaking at each pull of the engine. With the same voices, in the night, at each stop, the same men bustling around the mail car, the same whistle blast from the stationmaster.

He half opened his eyes, pulled at his pipe, which had gone out, and his glance rested on the man sitting in the opposite corner of the compartment. He might have seen this man too, in those days, in the train that took him home to his father's. He could have been the Count, or the owner of the château, the most important person of the village or of any little town.

He was wearing golf clothes of light tweed, and a rain-coat of the kind one sees only in certain very expensive shops. His hat was a green sportsman's hat, with a tiny pheasant's feather tucked inside the ribbon. In spite of the heat he had not taken off his fawn gloves, for such men never remove their gloves in a train or in a car. And despite the rain, there wasn't a spot of mud on his well-polished shoes.

He was probably sixty-five years old. He was already an elderly gentleman. Isn't it strange that men of that age take so much care over the details of their appearance? And that they still try to set themselves apart from the ordinary run of mortals?

His complexion was of that pink peculiar to the species, with a small silvery-white mustache marked with the yellow circle left by cigar-smoking.

2

His expression, however, did not have quite the assurance it should have had. From his corner Maigret watched the man, and he, on his part, glanced back several times and on two or three occasions appeared to be on the point of speaking. The train was setting off again, dirty and wet, into a dark world sprinkled with widely scattered lights, and now and then, at a grade crossing, one could make out someone on a bicycle waiting for the last car to pass.

Was it that Maigret was depressed? It was vaguer than that. He wasn't feeling quite himself. And anyway, these last three days, he had drunk too much, not with any pleasure but out of necessity.

He had been attending the International Police Congress, which, this year, was held at Bordeaux. It was April. When he had left Paris, where the winter had been long and monotonous, spring seemed to be not far off. But at Bordeaux it had rained all three days, with a cold wind that made your clothes cling to your body.

By chance, the few friends he usually met at these congresses, like Mr. Pyke, had not been there. Each country, it seemed, had contrived to send only young representatives, men of thirty to forty whom he had ever seen before. They had all shown great kindness to him, had been very deferential, as one is to an older man one respects and finds slightly old-fashioned.

Could that be it? Or had the unending rain put him in a bad humor? And all the wine that they had had to drink in the cellars they had been invited to visit by the Chamber of Commerce?

"Are you enjoying yourself?" his wife had asked on the telephone.

He had replied with a grunt.

"Try to rest a little. You looked tired when you left. A any rate, it will be ∧ change for you. Don't catch cold."

Perhaps he had suddenly felt old? Even their discussions, which almost all had to do with new scientific methods, hadn't interested him.

The banquet had taken place the previous evening. That morning there had been a final reception, at the Town Hall this time, and a lunch with lots to drink. He had promised Chabot that he would take advantage of not having to be in Paris until Monday morning and stop off to see him at Fontenay-le-Comte.

Chabot wasn't getting any younger either. They had been friends in the old days, when he had taken two years of medicine at the University of Nantes. Chabot himself had been a law student. They lived in the same boarding-house. On two or three Sundays he had gone with his friend to his mother's house in Fontenay.

And since then, across the years, they had seen each other perhaps ten times all told.

"When are you coming to visit me in Vendée?"

Madame Maigret had had a hand in it too

"Why don't you stop and see your friend Chabot on your way back from Bordeaux?"

He should have been at Fontenay two hours ago. He had taken the wrong train. At Niort, where he had waited a long time, having a number of glasses of brandy in the waiting room, he had hesitated to telephone for Chabot to come and fetch him by car.

He hadn't done so, in the end, because if Julien came to meet him, he would insist on Maigret's staying at his place, and the Chief Inspector hated sleeping in other people's houses.

He would go to the hotel. Once there and not before,

he would telephone. He had been wrong to make this detour instead of having these two days' holiday at home, on Boulevard Richard-Lenoir. Who knows? Perhaps in Paris it was no longer raining and spring had arrived at last.

"So, they have sent for you. . . ."

He jumped. Without realizing it, he must have gone on staring vaguely at his fellow passenger, and the latter had just made up his mind to speak to him. He seemed to be embarrassed about it himself. He felt he had to put on a slightly ironical tone of voice.

"I beg your pardon?"

"I said that I suspected they would call for someone like you."

Maigret still not seeming to understand, he continued:

"You are Chief Inspector Maigret, aren't you?"

The traveler became once more the man of the world, rose from his seat to introduce himself:

"Vernoux de Courçon."

"How do you do?"

"I recognized you immediately, from having often seen your photograph in the newspapers."

He said that rather as if he were apologizing for being one of those who read newspapers.

"It must happen to you often."

"What?"

"That people recognize you."

Maigret did not know what to reply. He hadn't yet come firmly down to earth. As for the man, little drops of sweat had appeared on his forehead, as if he had got himself into a situation from which he didn't know how to recover advantageously.

"Was it my friend Julien who telephoned you?"

5

"Do you mean Julien Chabot?"

"The Examining Magistrate. I'm only surprised that he said nothing to me about it when I met him this morning."

"I still don't understand."

Vernoux de Courçon looked at him more attentively, frowning.

"You mean to say that it's just by chance that you' coming to Fontenay-le-Comte?"

"Yes."

"Aren't you going to see Julien Chabot?"

"Yes, but . . ."

Maigret reddened suddenly furious with himself be cause he had just replied subserviently, as he used to do in the old days when he was addressed by people of this type, "the people from the château."

"Curious, isn't it?" said the other ironically.

"What is so curious?"

"That Chief Inspector Maigret, who has probably never set foot in Fontenay . . ."

"Has someone told you that?"

"I only presume so. At any rate, you have not been seen there often, and I have never heard any mention of it. It's curious, I say, that you should be arriving just at a time when the authorities are baffled by the most puzzling mystery that . . ."

Maigret struck a match, took little puffs at his pipe.

"I did part of my studies with Julien Chabot," he announced calmly. "Many times in the past, I have been a guest at his house on Rue Clemenceau."

"Indeed?"

Coldly, he repeated:

"Indeed."

6

"In that case, we shall surely see you tomorrow evening at my house on Rue Rabelais, where Chabot comes every Saturday for a game of bridge."

It was the last stop before Fontenay. Vernoux de Courçon had no luggage, only a chestnut-colored leather briefcase placed by his side on the seat.

"I shall be curious to see if you'll unveil the mystery. Chance or not, it is lucky for Chabot that you're here."

"Is his mother still alive?"

"As fit as ever."

The man got up to button his raincoat, smooth his gloves, adjust his hat. The train was slowing down, a string of lights went past, and men began to run along the platform.

"I am very glad to have met you. Tell Chabot that I look forward to seeing you both tomorrow evening."

Maigret merely replied with a nod and opened the door, took hold of his bag, which was heavy, and made his way to the exit without looking at the people he passed.

Chabot could not be expecting him on this train, which he had only caught by accident. In front of the station, Maigret looked down the length of Rue de la République, where it was pouring rain.

"Taxi, sir?"

He nodded.

"Hôtel de France?"

He said yes again, settled himself irritably into the corner. It was only nine o'clock in the evening, but there was no longer any sign of life in the town; only two or three cafés were still lighted. The door of the Hôtel de France was flanked by two palm trees in barrels painted green.

"Have you got a room?" *he asked the desk clerk.*

"With a single bed?"

"Yes. If it's possible, I would like something to eat."

The hotel was already half in darkness, like a church after vespers.

They had to go and ask in the kitchen, switch on two or three lights in the dining room.

To save going up to his room, he washed his hands in a porcelain washbasin.

"Some white wine?"

He was sick of all the white wine he had had to drink in Bordeaux.

"Haven't you got some beer?"

"Only in bottles."

"In that case, give me some red wine."

They had reheated some soup for him, and cut him some slices of ham. From his seat, he saw someone enter the lobby of the hotel, dripping wet. Finding no one to ask, this man peered into the dining room and seemed reassured to see the Chief Inspector there. He was a red-haired fellow of about forty, with large, ruddy cheeks and cameras slung over his shoulder outside his beige raincoat.

He shook his hat for the rain to drop off, came forward.

"First of all, do you mind if I take a photograph? I am the correspondent for *Ouest-Eclair* in this district. I just saw you at the station, but I wasn't able to catch up with you in time. So, they have sent for you to throw some light on the Courçon case."

A flash of light. A click.

"Superintendent Féron didn't tell us anything about you. Neither did the Examining Magistrate."

"I am not here on the Courçon case."

The young redhead smiled, the smile of someone in the know, who can't be fooled.

"But of course."

"Why of course?"

"You're not here *officially*. I understand. It doesn't mean that . . ."

"It means nothing at all!"

"The proof is that Féron's told me he is hurrying over."

"Who's Féron?"

"The Fontenay Police Superintendent. When I spotted you at the station, I dived into a telephone booth and called him up. He told me he would meet me here."

"Here?"

"Certainly. Where else would you stay?"

Maigret emptied his glass, wiped his mouth, growled:

"Who is this Vernoux de Courçon with whom I traveled from Niort?"

"Yes, he was on the train. He's the brother-in-law."

"Whose brother-in-law?"

"Courçon's, the murdered man's."

A short brown-haired figure now entered the hotel and at once noticed the two men in the dining room.

"Hello, Féron," called the reporter.

"Good evening to you. Forgive me, Chief Inspector. Nobody told me of your arrival, which explains why I wasn't at the station. I was having a quick snack, after a harassing day, when . . ."

He pointed to the redhead.

"I hurried and . . ."

"I was telling this young man," said Maigret, pushing away his plate and grasping his pipe, "that I have nothing to do with this Courçon affair of yours. I've come to

Fontenay-le-Comte, by purest chance, to pay a visit to my old friend Chabot and . . ."

"Does he know that you're here?"

"He was supposed to be expecting me on the four o'clock train. Since he didn't see me, he probably thought that I wouldn't come until tomorrow, or that I wouldn't come at all."

Maigret rose.

"And now, with your leave, I shall go and call on him before going to bed."

Both the Superintendent and the reporter looked disconcerted.

"You really know nothing?"

"Absolutely nothing."

"You haven't read the newspapers?"

"The past three days, the organizers of the Police Congress and the Bordeaux Chamber of Commerce haven't left us a moment to ourselves."

They exchanged dubious glances.

"You know where the Magistrate lives?"

"Yes, indeed. That is, if the town hasn't changed since I paid my last visit."

They couldn't bring themselves to let him go. On the sidewalk they stood on either side of him.

"Gentlemen, I must bid you farewell."

The reporter persisted:

"Have you no statement to make for *Ouest-Eclair*?"

"None. Good night, gentlemen."

He reached Rue de la République, crossed the bridge, and passed hardly anyone as he climbed the hill to Chabot's house. Chabot lived in an old house, which in his youth had excited Maigret's admiration. It was still the same, of gray stone with four steps and tall windows

10

with small panes. A little light filtered between the curtains. He rang the bell, heard quick, short steps on the blue flagstones of the hallway. A peephole was opened in the door.

"Is Monsieur Chabot at home?" he asked.

"Who is it?"

"Chief Inspector Maigret."

"Is that you, Monsieur Maigret?"

He had recognized the voice of Rose, the Chabots' maid, who had been with them for thirty years.

"I'll let you in right away. Just wait while I take off the chain."

At the same time, she called inside the house.

"Monsieur Julien! It's your friend Monsieur Maigret. . . . Come in, Monsieur Maigret. . . . Monsieur Julien went to the station this afternoon. He was disappointed not to find you. How did you come?"

"By train."

"Do you mean that you took the local train this evening?"

A door had opened. In the beam of orange-shaded light stood a tall, thin man, slightly stooping, wearing a maroon velvet smoking jacket.

"Is that you?" he said.

"Indeed it is. I missed the good train. So I took the bad one."

"Your luggage?"

"It's at the hotel."

"How silly! I will have to have it collected. We agreed that you would stay here."

"No, wait, Julien. . . ."

It was funny. It was an effort to call his old friend by his first name, and it sounded strange.

"Come in. I hope you haven't eaten?"

"Yes, I have. At the Hôtel de France."

"Shall I inform Madame?" asked Rose.

Maigret intervened.

"I suppose she's in bed?"

"She has just gone upstairs. But she won't be in bed before eleven o'clock or midnight. I . . ."

"Don't you dare. I refuse to let her be disturbed. I shall see your mother tomorrow morning."

"She won't be pleased."

Maigret calculated that Madame Chabot would be at least seventy-eight. Deep down, he was sorry he had come. Nevertheless, he hung up his overcoat, which was heavy with rain, on the old coatrack, followed Julien into his study, while Rose, who was herself in her sixties, waited for orders.

"What will you have? A brandy?"

"Yes, if you wish."

Rose understood the Magistrate's unspoken instructions and disappeared. The smell of the house had not changed, and this too was something Maigret had envied in the past, the smell of a well-kept house, where the floors were waxed and the cooking was good.

He would have sworn that not a single article of furniture had changed position.

"Sit down. I am very glad to see you."

He would have been tempted to say that Chabot hadn't changed either. His features, his expression, were just the same. Because both of them had aged, it was difficult for Maigret to judge the effect of the passing years. He was, just the same, struck by some kind of lifelessness, uncertainty, a little feebleness that he had never observed before in his friend.

Had he been like that in the old days? Had Maigret simply not noticed it?

"Cigar?"

There was a pile of boxes on the mantelpiece.

"Still the pipe."

"Of course, I had forgotten. I myself haven't smoked for twelve years."

"Doctor's orders?"

"No. One fine day I said to myself that it was stupid to cause a lot of smoke and . . ."

Rose entered with a tray on which there was a bottle, covered with fine cellar dust, and a single crystal glass.

"Don't you drink any more either?"

"I gave it up at the same time. Just a little wine with a dash of water at mealtime. You haven't changed."

"Don't you think so?"

"You seem to enjoy wonderful health. I'm really delighted that you have come."

Why did he not seem altogether sincere?

"You have promised to stop here so often, then put it off at the last moment, that I confess I gave up counting on you too much."

"Everything works out in the end, you see!"

"Your wife?"

"She's very well."

"She didn't accompany you?"

"She doesn't like congresses."

"Did it go off well?"

"We all drank a lot, talked a lot, ate a lot."

"I do less and less traveling."

He lowered his voice, for footsteps could be heard on the floor above. "With my mother, it's difficult. Besides, I cannot leave her alone now."

"Is she still as fit as ever?"

"She doesn't change. Her sight is the only thing that has weakened a little. It distresses her not to be able to thread her needles nowadays, but she obstinately refuses to wear glasses."

There was the feeling that he had his mind on other things, as he watched Maigret in rather the same way Vernoux de Courçon had watched him on the train.

"Have you heard the news?"

"What about?"

"What's been happening here."

"I haven't read a paper for almost a week. But I traveled just now with a certain Vernoux de Courçon, who calls himself a friend of yours."

"Hubert?"

"I don't know. A man of about sixty-five."

"That's Hubert."

Not a sound came from the town. One could hear only the rain beating against the windowpanes and, from time to time, the crackling of the logs in the fireplace. Julien Chabot's father, before him, had been Examining Magistrate at Fontenay-le-Comte, and the study had not changed in passing from father to son.

"In that case, you must have been told . . ."

"Almost nothing. A journalist descended upon me with his camera in the hotel dining room."

"A man with red hair?"

"Yes."

"That's Lomel. What did he say to you?"

"He was convinced that I was here to take part in some case or other. I hadn't had time to disabuse him before the local Police Superintendent arrived as well."

"In fact, by now the whole town knows you're here?"

14

"Does that worry you?"

Chabot barely managed to hide his hesitation.

"No . . . it's only . . ."

"Only what?"

"Nothing. It's very complicated. You have never lived in a country town like Fontenay."

"I lived at Luçon for more than a year, you know!"

"There was no case of the kind I have on my hands now."

"I remember a certain murder, at L'Aiguillon . . ."

"That's true. I was forgetting."

It was actually a case in the course of which Maigret had found himself obliged to arrest, on a charge of murder, an ex-magistrate whom everybody considered perfectly respectable.

"That wasn't so serious, however. You will realize that tomorrow morning. I wouldn't be surprised if the Paris newspapermen arrived on the first train."

"A murder?"

"Two."

"Vernoux de Courçon's brother-in-law."

"You see, you do know!"

"That's all I've been told."

"Yes, his brother-in-law, Robert de Courçon, was murdered four days ago. That alone would have been enough to make a fuss about. The day before yesterday, it happened to the widow Gibon."

"Who's she?"

"Nobody of importance. Far from it. An old woman who lived alone right at the end of Rue des Loges."

"What's the connection between the two crimes?"

"Both were committed in the same way, probably with the same weapon."

"A revolver?"

"No. A blunt instrument, as we say in reports. A piece of lead piping, or a tool like a wrench."

"Is that all?"

"Isn't that enough? . . . Hush!"

The door opened silently, and a very small, very thin woman, dressed in black, came forward with her hand outstretched.

"There you are, Jules!"

How many years was it since anyone had called him by that name?

"My son went to the station. When he returned, he assured me that you wouldn't be coming and I retired upstairs. Haven't they given you any dinner?"

"He dined at the hotel, Mama."

"What do you mean, at the hotel?"

"He is staying at the Hôtel de France. He refuses to . . ."

"Oh, no, never! I shall not allow you to . . ."

"Madame, please. There's all the more reason for me to stay at the hotel now that the reporters are already after me. If I accepted your invitation, tomorrow morning, if not tonight, they would be hanging on your doorbell. Besides, it's better that nobody should suppose I'm here at your son's request. . . ."

It was this, after all, that was bothering the Magistrate, and Maigret saw it confirmed in his face.

"They will say that anyway!"

"I shall deny it. This case, or, rather, these cases are no concern of mine. I haven't the slightest intention of being involved in them."

Had Chabot been afraid that he would interfere in

things that didn't concern him? Or had he imagined that Maigret, with his occasionally somewhat personal methods, might put him in a delicate situation?

The Chief Inspector had arrived at an awkward moment.

"I wonder, Mama, if Maigret isn't right."

And, turning to his old friend:

"You see, this isn't an ordinary case. Robert de Courçon, who's been murdered, was a well-known man, more or less closely related to all the big families in the district. His brother-in-law Vernoux is also an important figure. After the first crime, rumors began to get around. Then the widow Gibon was murdered, and that slightly altered the course of the gossip. But . . ."

"But . . . ?"

"It's difficult to explain to you. The Police Superintendent is in charge of the investigations. He's a good fellow and he knows the town, though he comes from the Midi, from Arles, I believe. The Poitiers Flying Squad is also on the spot. So, in my position . . ."

The old lady had sat down, as though she were paying a call, on the edge of a chair, and was listening to her son speaking as she might have listened to the sermon at high mass.

"Two murders in three days is a lot in a town of eight thousand inhabitants. Some people are getting frightened. It's not simply because of the rain tonight that you don't meet anyone in the streets."

"What does the public think?"

"Some maintain it's a lunatic."

"There was no robbery?"

"In neither case. And in both cases the murderer was

able to get himself let in the door without his victims being suspicious. It's a clue. And it's about the only one we've got."

"No fingerprints?"

"None. If it's a lunatic, he'll probably commit other murders."

"I see. And you, what do you think?"

"Nothing. I am trying to puzzle it out. I'm worried."

"By what?"

"It's still too confused for me to explain. I have a terrible responsibility on my shoulders."

He said this like an overworked official. And it was indeed an official Maigret had before him now, a small-town official living in terror of making a false step.

Had the Chief Inspector too grown like this with age? He felt older himself, because of his friend.

"I wonder if I wouldn't do better to take the first train back to Paris. After all, I only came to Fontenay to say 'How do you do.' That's done. My presence here may cause complications for you."

"What do you mean?"

Chabot's first reaction had *not* been one of protest.

"Already the redhead and the local Superintendent are convinced that you have called me to the rescue. They will say that you're scared, that you don't know how to deal with it, that . . ."

"Oh, no."

The Magistrate rejected this notion only rather weakly.

"I will not allow you to leave. I may still receive my friends as I please."

"My son is right, Jules. And for my part, I think you should stay with us."

"Maigret prefers to have his freedom of movement, is that it?"

"I have my own habits."

"I don't insist."

"It will still be better if I leave tomorrow morning."

Perhaps Chabot was going to agree. The telephone rang, and its ring was not like any other, a quaint sound.

"Will you excuse me?"

Chabot lifted the receiver.

"Chabot, Examining Magistrate, speaking."

The way in which he said that was yet another sign, and Maigret forced himself not to smile.

"Who? . . . Ah, yes . . . It's you, Féron. . . . What? . . . Gobillard? . . . Where? . . . At the corner of the Champ de Mars and . . . I'll come immediately. . . . Yes. He's here. . . . I don't know. . . . Tell them not to touch a thing until I arrive."

His mother looked at him, her hand held to her breast.

"Another one?" she stammered.

He nodded.

"Gobillard."

He explained to Maigret:

"An old drunkard, whom everybody in Fontenay knows because he spends the best part of his days fishing beside the bridge. They have just found him on the sidewalk, dead."

"Murdered?"

"His skull's been fractured, like the other two, most likely with the same instrument."

He had risen, opened the door, unhooked from the stand an old trenchcoat and a battered hat, which he probably used only on rainy days.

"Are you coming?"

"Do you think I ought to accompany you?"

"Now that it's known you're here, they would wonder why I didn't bring you. Two crimes was a lot. With a third, the town is going to be frightened out of its wits."

As they were going out, a nervous little hand seized Maigret's sleeve and old Mama whispered in his ear:

"Look after him, Jules! He is so conscientious that he doesn't realize the danger."

2

With such a degree of obstinacy, of violence, in it as this, the rain was no longer just rain, or the wind a mere icy wind; it was becoming a vicious conspiracy of the elements, and already, on the poorly sheltered platform of the station at Niort, harassed by this winter whose final convulsions seemed determined not to end, Maigret had been put in mind of a beast which refuses to die and struggles to bite, to the very last.

It was no use now trying to protect oneself. Water was not only pouring from the sky, but also falling from drainpipes in large, cold splashes, and running down the doors of houses and along the sidewalks, where streams of it reared like a torrent. There was water all over one, on one's face, down one's neck, into one's shoes, and even into the pockets of clothes, which were past drying out between excursions.

They were walking against the wind, without speaking, leaning forward, the Magistrate in his old raincoat, with its skirts flapping like flags, Maigret in his overcoat, which weighed two hundred pounds. After a few paces, the tobacco sizzled out with a sputter in the Chief Inspector's pipe.

Here and there, the odd lighted window could be seen, but not many of them. After the bridge, they passed the windows of the Café de la Poste, and were aware that people were watching them over the tops of the curtains; the door opened after they had gone on a bit farther, and they heard footsteps, voices, behind them.

The murder had taken place very near there. At Fontenay, nothing is ever very far away, and it is usually pointless to take your car out of the garage. A short street struck off to the right, joining Rue de la République to the Champ de Mars. In front of the third or fourth house a group of people was standing on the sidewalk, near the headlights of an ambulance, some of them holding flashlights in their hands.

A little man detached himself from the group—Superintendent Féron, who almost put his foot in it by addressing Maigret rather than Chabot.

"I telephoned you immediately from the Café de la Poste. I also telephoned the Public Prosecutor."

A human form was lying across the sidewalk. One hand hung in the gutter, and the gleam of his pale skin could be seen between his black shoes and the bottom of his trousers. Gobillard, the dead man, was wearing no socks. His hat lay a yard away. Féron directed his flashlight on the face, and, as Maigret and the Magistrate were both bending over, there was a flash, a click, then the voice of the red-haired journalist asking:

"One more, please. A bit closer, Monsieur Maigret."

The Chief Inspector stepped back, groaning. Near the body, two or three people were observing him; then, quite separate, five or six yards away, there was a second group, bigger in number, where they were talking in whispers.

Chabot inquired, in a manner both official and exhausted:

"Who found him?"

And Féron answered, pointing to one of the nearest figures standing by, "Doctor Vernoux."

Did he too belong to the same family as the man in the train? As far as one could judge in the darkness, he was much younger. Perhaps thirty-five? He was tall, with a long nervous face, wore glasses, across which drops of rain were sliding.

Chabot and he shook hands mechanically, in the manner of men who meet every day and even several times a day.

The doctor explained in a low voice:

"I was calling on a friend, on the other side of the square. I saw something on the sidewalk. I bent over. He was already dead. To save time, I dashed to the Café de la Poste, from where I telephoned the Superintendent."

Other faces were caught one after another in the beams of the flashlights, always with streaks of rain haloing them.

"Is that you, Jussieux?"

A handshake. These men knew each other like pupils in the same class at school.

"I was in the café just now. We were playing bridge and we've all come . . ."

The Magistrate, remembering Maigret, who was keeping in the background, proceeded to introduce him:

"Doctor Jussieux, a friend of mine. Chief Inspector Maigret . . ."

Jussieux was explaining:

"Same methods as with the other two. A violent blow on the top of the skull. The weapon slipped slightly to the left, this time. Gobillard too has been attacked from in front, without attempting to protect himself at all."

"Drunk?"

"You have only to lean over and sniff. At this time of night, besides, since you know him well . . ."

Maigret was listening with only half an ear. Lomel, the redheaded journalist, who had just taken a second picture, was trying to draw him to one side. What struck the Chief Inspector was something rather difficult to define.

The smaller of the two groups, the one standing near the corpse, appeared to be composed only of men who knew each other, who belonged to a particular set: the Magistrate, the two doctors, the men who, doubtless, had just been playing bridge with Dr. Jussieux, all of whom were probably local worthies.

The other group, less in the light, was not keeping so quiet. Without, strictly speaking, showing it, it emanated a kind of hostility. There were even two or three derisive snorts.

A dark car had just parked behind the ambulance and a man got out, who stopped short on recognizing Maigret.

"You here, Chief!"

He did not appear too pleased to meet the Chief Inspector. It was Chabiron, a Flying Squad detective, for the past few years attached to the Poitiers force.

"Did they send for you?"

"I'm just here by chance."

"That's what they call striking it lucky, eh?"

He too laughed derisively.

"I was busy patrolling the town in my jalopy, which explains why it took so long to inform me. Who is it?"

Féron, the Police Superintendent, explained to him:

"A certain Gobillard, a fellow who goes around Fontenay once or twice a week collecting rabbitskins. He also buys up hides of cattle and sheepskins from the municipal slaughterhouse. He has a cart and an old horse, and he lives in a hut outside town. He spends most of his time fishing near the bridge, using the most disgusting bait, marrow, fat, chicken guts, clotted blood. . . ."

Chabiron must have been a fisherman.

"Does he catch any fish?"

"He's practically the only man who does. Every evening he goes from bar to bar drinking a jug of red wine in each, until he reaches his limit."

"Ever any trouble?"

"Never."

"Married?"

"He lived alone with his horse and a large number of cats."

Chabiron turned to Maigret:

"What do you think, Chief?"

"I don't think anything."

"Three in one week; it's not bad for a little spot like this."

"What are we to do?" Féron asked the Magistrate.

"I don't think it's necessary to wait for the Prosecutor. Wasn't he home?"

"No. His wife's trying to get him on the phone."

"I think we might move the body to the morgue."

He turned to Dr. Vernoux.

"You saw nothing else, heard nothing?"

"Not a thing. I was walking quickly, my hands in my pockets. I all but stumbled over him."

"Is your father at home?"

"He returned this evening from Niort; he was eating when I left."

As far as Maigret could understand, this was the son of the Vernoux de Courçon with whom he had traveled in the local train.

"You can take him away, the rest of you."

The journalist would not leave Maigret alone.

"Are you going to take charge of it, this time?"

"Certainly not."

"Not even in a private capacity?"

"No."

"Aren't you curious?"

"No."

"Do you too believe in these being the crimes of a lunatic?"

Chabot and Dr. Vernoux, who had heard, looked at each other, still with that air of belonging to the same set, of knowing each other so well that words are no longer necessary.

It was natural. It exists everywhere. Rarely, nevertheless, had Maigret had such a strong sense of a clique. In a little town like this there are, of course, the local worthies, few in number, who, through force of circumstances, meet each other, if only in the street, several times a day.

Then there are the others, those, for example, who were gathered together to one side and seemed discontented.

Without the Chief Inspector's having asked at all, Chabiron was explaining to him:

"A couple of us have come over. Levras, who was my partner, had to leave this morning, because his wife's expecting a baby any time now. I'm doing what I can. I'm tackling the case from all angles at once. But as for getting those people over there to talk . . ."

It was the first group, the local worthies, whom he indicated with a jerk of his chin. His sympathies were obviously with the others.

"The Police Superintendent too does his best. He has only four policemen at his disposal. They've been working on it all day. How many have you out on patrol at the moment, Féron?"

"Three."

As if to confirm his statement, a bicyclist in uniform stopped by the curb and shook the rain from his shoulders.

"Anything?"

"I've checked the papers of the half-dozen people I've met. I'll give you the list. They all had good reasons for being out of doors."

"Will you come back home for a moment?" Chabot asked Maigret.

He hesitated. He chose to do so only because he wanted something to drink in order to get warm again, and he didn't expect he would be able to get anything at the hotel.

"I'll come along with you," Dr. Vernoux announced. "That is, if I'm not intruding?"

"Not at all."

This time, they had the wind behind them and were

able to talk. The ambulance had departed with Gobillard's body, and its red taillight could be seen going toward Place Viète.

"I haven't properly introduced you. Vernoux is the son of Hubert Vernoux, whom you met on the train. He's a qualified doctor, but doesn't practice, and is chiefly concerned with research."

"Research! . . . ." the doctor protested half-heartedly.

"He was a resident for two years at Sainte-Anne; now he's keenly interested in psychiatry, and two or three times a week he goes to Niort lunatic asylum."

"Do you believe these three crimes are the work of a madman?" asked Maigret, more out of politeness than anything else.

What he had just heard had not made him take kindly to Vernoux, since he didn't care for amateurs.

"It's more than likely, if not certain."

"Do you know any mad people in Fontenay?"

"There are some everywhere, but usually one only discovers them at the critical moment."

"I suppose it couldn't be a woman?"

"Why not?"

"Because of the force with which the blows have been struck on each occasion. It can't be easy to commit a murder like that, three times, without ever needing to strike twice."

"In the first place, many women are as strong as men. Again, when you're dealing with lunatics . . ."

They had already arrived.

"Anything you want to talk about, Vernoux?"

"Not for the moment."

"Shall I see you tomorrow?"

"Almost certainly."

Chabot searched in his pocket for the key. In the hallway, he and Maigret shook themselves so that the rain would fall off their clothes, and immediately there were trails of water on the flagstones. The two women, mother and maid, were waiting in a badly lit living room, which looked onto the street.

"You can go to bed, Mama. There's nothing more to be done tonight, except to ask the police station to put all available men out on patrol."

Only then did she decide to go upstairs.

"I feel really ashamed that you're not staying with us, Jules!"

"I promise you that if I stay more than twenty-four hours, which I doubt, I shall be making demands on your hospitality."

They returned to the tranquil atmosphere of the study, where the bottle of brandy was still in its place. Maigret helped himself and went to stand with his back to the fire, his glass in his hand.

He sensed that Chabot was ill at ease, that it was for this reason he had brought him back. Before anything else, the Magistrate telephoned the police station.

"Is that you, Lieutenant? You were in bed? I'm sorry to disturb you at this hour . . ."

A clock with a bronzed dial, on which the hands could hardly be seen, showed half past eleven.

"Yet another one, yes . . . Gobillard . . . In the street, this time . . . And from the front, yes . . . They've already taken him to the morgue. . . . Jussieux is probably busy doing the post-mortem now, but there's no reason why we should learn anything from it. . . . Have you some men handy? . . . I think it would be a good thing if they patrolled the town, not so much tonight as in the early hours

29

of the morning, to reassure the townspeople. . . . You understand? . . . Yes . . . I felt that just now too. . . Thank you, Lieutenant."

Replacing the receiver, he murmured:

"A charming fellow. He graduated from Saumur . . ."

He must have realized what that signified—always a question of class!—and blushed slightly.

"You see! I'm doing what I can. It must seem childish to you. We probably give you the impression of being desperately old-fashioned. But we don't have the advantages of an organization such as you are used to in Paris. For fingerprints, for example, I'm obliged every time to send for an expert from Poitiers. So it is with everything. The local police are more used to petty offenses than to crimes. The Poitiers detectives, for their part, don't know the people of Fontenay. . . ."

He went on after a pause:

"I'd have given anything, with only three years left before my retirement, not to have been saddled with a case like this. In fact, we're about the same age. You too in three years' time . . ."

"Me too."

"Have you any plans?"

"I've even bought a little house in the country already, on the banks of the Loire."

"You'll be bored."

"Are you bored, here?"

"It's not the same. I was born here. My father was born here. I know everyone there is to know."

"The townspeople don't seem very happy."

"You've barely arrived and you've already realized that? It's true. I think it's inevitable. One crime, and it wasn't so bad. Especially the first one."

30

"Why?"

"Because it happens to have been Robert de Courçon."

"Wasn't he liked?"

The Magistrate did not reply right away. He appeared to be choosing his words first.

"Actually, the ordinary people hardly knew him, except by sight."

"Married? Children?"

"An old bachelor. An eccentric, but a good fellow. If he had been the only one, the people would have remained fairly cool about it. Just the little excitement that always accompanies a crime. But, one after the other, there's been the widow Gibon, and now Gobillard. Tomorrow, I'm prepared to find . . ."

"It's already begun."

"What?"

"The group that was keeping to one side, the ordinary people, I suppose, and those who'd come out of the Café de la Poste seemed rather hostile to me."

"It won't stop at that. However . . ."

"Is the town very left-wing?"

"Yes and no. It's not altogether that, either."

"The Vernouxs are unpopular?"

"Have you been told that?"

To gain time, Chabot asked:

"Won't you sit down? Have another glass? I'll try to explain to you. It's not easy. You know the Vendée, if only by repute. For a long time, the only people who counted were the owners of châteaux, counts, viscounts, anyone who had a 'de' to his name, who lived among themselves and formed a closed society. They still exist, almost all impoverished, and they hardly matter any longer. A few of them still continue nevertheless to put up a certain show, and they are regarded with a kind of pity. Do you understand?"

"It's the same in all country districts."

"Now, others have taken their place."

"Vernoux?"

"Well, you have seen him; guess what his father did."

"Haven't the least idea! What do you mean?"

"Cattle dealer. The grandfather was a farm hand. Father Vernoux bought up the livestock in the district and drove them to Paris, in whole herds, along the roads. He made a lot of money. He was a brute, always half-drunk, and, what's more, he died of delirium tremens. His son . . ."

"Hubert? The one on the train?"

"Yes. He was sent to college. I believe he did one year at a university. In the last years of his life, the father started buying farms and land as well as cattle, and it was that business Hubert continued."

"In fact, he's a dealer in real estate."

"Yes. He has his office near the station, the large freestone house; that was where he lived before he married."

"He married a nobleman's daughter?"

"In one way, yes. But not exactly, either. She was a Courçon. Does this interest you?"

"Very much!"

"It will give you a better idea of the town. The Courçons were really called Courçon-Lagrange. Originally, they were just Lagranges, who added Courçon to their name when they bought the Château de Courçon. That happened three or four generations ago. I can't remember what the founder of the dynasty sold. Probably cattle also, or scrap iron. But that was all forgotten by the time

Hubert Vernoux arrived on the scene. The children and grandchildren no longer did any work. Robert de Courçon, the one who's been murdered, was recognized by the aristocracy and he was the most expert man in the country around here on matters of heraldry. He's written several works on the subject. He had two sisters, Isabelle and Lucile. Isabelle married Vernoux, who at once began to sign himself Vernoux de Courçon. Have you followed me?"

"It's not too difficult! I suppose that, at the time of this marriage, the Courçons had descended the scale again and found themselves without money?"

"Pretty much. They still had a mortgaged château in the forest of Mervent and the house on Rue Rabelais, which is the handsomest residence in the town, and which they've several times tried to get listed as a historical monument. You'll be seeing it."

"Is Hubert Vernoux still a real-estate dealer?"

"He has heavy liabilities. Lucile, his wife's elder sister, lives with them. His son, Alain, the doctor, whom you've just met, refuses to practice and devotes himself to research, which brings in nothing."

"Married?"

"He married a Mademoiselle de Cadeuils, from the real nobility this time, who's borne him three children already. The youngest is eight months old."

"They live with the father?"

"The house is large enough, as you'll realize. That's not all. In addition to Alain, Hubert has a daughter, Adeline, who married a certain Paillet, whom she met while on holiday at Royan. What he does for a living, I don't know, but I have reason to believe that it's Hubert Vernoux who provides for their needs. Most of the time they

33

live in Paris. Now and then, they turn up for a few days or a few weeks, and I suppose that means that they're hard up. Do you understand now?"

"What have I got to understand?"

Chabot smiled mournfully, which for a moment reminded Maigret of his former comrade.

"It's true, I'm talking to you as though you came from here. You've seen Vernoux. He outsquires all the squires of the neighborhood. As for his wife and her sister, they seem to contrive with all their skill to make themselves odious to the ordinary run of people. The whole thing constitutes a clique."

"And this clique is on visiting terms with only a small proportion of the people."

Chabot blushed for the second time that evening.

"Inevitably," he murmured, rather as if he were guilty.

"So that the Vernouxs, the Courçons, and their friends have become a world apart in the town."

"You've guessed right. Through the very nature of my position, I am obliged to see them. And, basically, they are not so odious as they appear to be. Hubert Vernoux, for example, is in fact, I would swear, a man overwhelmed with worries. He has been very rich. He is less so now, and I even wonder if he still is at all, because, since the majority of farmers have bought their own properties, the land business is no longer what it used to be. Hubert is weighed down with expenses, is obliged to provide for all his relatives. As for Alain, whom I know better, he's a young man obsessed with one idea."

"What's that?"

"You'd better hear about it. At the same time, you will learn why, just now, in the street, he and I exchanged anxious glances. I've told you that Hubert Vernoux's father died of delirium tremens. On the mother's side, that is to say the Courçons, the antecedents were no better. Old Courçon committed suicide in circumstances sufficiently mysterious for them to have been hushed up. Hubert had a brother, Basile, of whom they never speak, who killed himself at the age of seventeen. It seems that, however far back you go, there have been lunatics or eccentrics in the family."

Maigret was listening, all the while lazily smoking his pipe, and taking a sip, every now and again, from his glass.

"That's the reason why Alain studied medicine, and went to Sainte-Anne as a resident. It's said, and it's plausible, that most medical men specialize in the illnesses with which they believe they themselves are threatened.

"Alain is obsessed by the idea that he belongs to a family of lunatics. According to him, Lucile, his aunt, is half-mad. He hasn't said so to me, but I'm convinced that he keeps looking for signs, not only in his father and mother, but also in his own children."

"Is it known in the locality?"

"Some people talk about it. In little towns, there's always a lot of gossip and a certain amount of mistrust of people who don't live exactly like everybody else."

"They talked about it after the first crime particularly?"

Chabot hesitated only a second, nodded his head.

"Why?"

"Because they knew, or thought they did, that Hubert Vernoux and his brother-in-law, Courçon, didn't get on together. Perhaps also because they lived directly opposite one another."

"Did they see each other?"

"I wonder what you're going to think of us. I imagine no similar situation could exist in Paris."

In fact, the Examining Magistrate was ashamed of a milieu that was somewhat his own, since he lived in it year in, year out.

"I told you that the Courçons were in financial straits when Isabelle married Hubert Vernoux. It's been Hubert who's given his brother-in-law, Robert, an allowance. And Robert's never forgiven him for it. When he mentioned him, he would say sarcastically:

"*'My brother-in-law, the millionaire.'*

"Or else:

"*'I'll go and ask the Rich Man.'*

"He wouldn't set foot in the big house on Rue Rabelais; he could follow all the comings and goings from his own windows. He lived opposite in a smaller house, but a decent one, where he had a daily cleaning woman. He polished his boots and got his meals himself, ostentatiously setting off to do his shopping dressed like a lord on the round of his estates, and he would bring home his bunches of leeks or asparagus as if they were trophies. He must have imagined it would make Hubert angry."

"Did Hubert get angry?"

"I don't know. Possibly. He continued to support him nonetheless. Several times they've been seen, when they met in the street, exchanging politely cutting remarks. A small detail, which is no fabrication: Robert de Courçon never drew the curtains of his windows, with the result that the family opposite could see how he lived all the time. Some people make out that he occasionally put out his tongue at them.

"The next step is to make out that Vernoux had him got rid of, or killed him in a fit of temper. . . ."

"That has been said?"

"Yes."

"Have you thought so too?"

"Professionally, I can reject no hypothesis *a priori*."

Maigret could not help smiling at this pompous phrase.

"Have you questioned Vernoux?"

"I haven't summoned him to my office, if that's what you mean. After all, there haven't been sufficient grounds for suspecting a man like him."

He had said:

"A man like him."

And he realized that he had given himself away, that this was acknowledging that he was more or less part of the clique. The whole evening, this visit from Maigret, were probably torture for him. Nor was it a pleasant experience for the Chief Inspector, although, by now, he no longer felt the same desire to leave.

"I met him in the street, as I do every morning, and asked him a few questions, without appearing to do so."

"What did he say?"

"That he had not left his rooms that evening."

"At what time was the crime committed?"

"The first one? About the same time as today, around ten o'clock in the evening."

"What are they usually doing at the Vernouxs' at that time?"

"Apart from bridge on Saturdays, which brings them all together in the living room, each one leads his own life without bothering about the rest."

"Vernoux doesn't sleep in the same room as his wife?"

"He would regard that as middle-class. Each one has his or her own suite of rooms, on different floors. Isabelle is on the second, Hubert in a wing of the ground floor, which looks onto the courtyard. Alain's household occupies the third floor, and the aunt, Lucile, two rooms on the fourth, which are attics. When the daughter and her husband are there . . ."

"Are they there at present?"

"No. They're expected in a few days."

"How many servants?"

"A married couple, who've been with them for twenty or thirty years, and two fairly young maids as well."

"Where do they sleep?"

"In the other wing on the ground floor. You'll see the house. It's almost a château."

"With a way out at back?"

"There's a door in the wall of the courtyard, which leads into a lane."

"So that anyone can go in or out without being seen?"

"Probably."

"You haven't checked?"

Chabot was on the rack and, because he felt himself at fault, he raised his voice, all but furious with his friend.

"You're talking the way some of the common people do here. If I had gone to question the servants, when I hadn't any evidence, not the slightest clue, the whole town would have been convinced that Hubert Vernoux or his son was guilty."

"His son?"

"He too, definitely! Because, from the moment he stopped work and became interested in psychiatry, there have been people who regard him as mad. He doesn't go to either of the town's two cafés, doesn't play billiards or belotte, doesn't run after girls, and sometimes, in the street, he will stop abruptly to stare at someone, his eyes enlarged by the lenses of his glasses. They're so disliked that . . ."

"You're defending them?"

"No. I must keep my detachment, and, in a country town, it's not always easy. I'm trying to be fair. I too thought that the first crime was probably a family affair. I studied the matter from all aspects. The fact that there was no robbery, that Robert de Courçon did not attempt to defend himself, worried me. And doubtless I would have taken certain measures if . . ."

"Wait a moment. You haven't asked the police to follow Hubert Vernoux and his son?"

"In Paris, that's practicable. Not here. Everyone knows our four unfortunate policemen. As for the Poitiers detectives, they were spotted before they even got out of their car! It's seldom there are more than ten people at any one time in the street. You mean that, under such conditions, someone should be followed without his suspecting it?"

He calmed down suddenly.

"Forgive me. I'm talking so loud I will wake my mother. It's just that I'd like you to understand my position. Until there is proof to the contrary, the Vernouxs are innocent. I would swear to it that they are. The second crime, two days after the first, has almost proved it. Hubert Vernoux could be driven to kill his brother-in-law, to strike him in a moment of rage. He had no reason to take himself off to the end of Rue des Loges in order to assassinate the widow Gibon, whom he probably didn't know."

"Who is she?"

"A retired midwife, whose husband, long since dead, was a policeman. She lived alone, half-crippled, in a three-room house.

"Not only has there been the old Gibon woman, but Gobillard this evening. The Vernouxs knew him, all right, as the whole of Fontenay did. In every town in France, there's at least one drunkard of his kind, who becomes a sort of popular figure.

"If you can cite me a single reason for killing a fellow of that sort . . ."

"Suppose he had seen something?"

"And the widow Gibon, who never left her house any longer? Would she have gone to Rue Rabelais, after ten o'clock at night, to witness the crime through the windows? No, come, come! I know the methods of criminal investigation. I didn't attend the Bordeaux Congress, and I may be a little behindhand, perhaps, on the latest scientific discoveries, but I think I know my profession and carry it out conscientiously. The three victims belonged to completely different backgrounds, and there was not the slightest connection between them. All three were killed in the same manner and, by the look of the injuries, one might conclude with the same weapon, and all three were attacked from in front, which presupposes that they had no suspicions. If it is a lunatic, it's not a wild or raving one, of whom everyone would steer clear. It's therefore what I might call a clearheaded lunatic, who's following a definite line of activity and is sufficiently circumspect to take precautions."

"Alain Vernoux hasn't fully explained his presence in the town, this evening, in such pouring rain."

"He said he was going to see a friend on the other side of the Champ de Mars."

"He didn't give any name."

"Because it's not necessary. I know that he often goes to visit a certain Georges Vassal, a bachelor, whom he knew at college. Even without that knowledge, I wouldn't have been surprised."

"Why not?"

"Because the case fascinates him even more than me, for more personal reasons. I'm not suggesting that he suspects his father, but I don't think he's far from it. Some weeks ago, he talked to me about him and the family failings . . ."

"Just like that?"

"No. He was coming back from La Roche-sur-Yon and was quoting a case that he had been studying. It concerned a man in his sixties, who up to that time had behaved normally, but who, on the day when he should have presented the long-promised dowry to his daughter, went off his head. It was not immediately detected."

"In other words, you're saying that Alain Vernoux might have been wandering around Fontenay at night on the lookout for the murderer?"

The Examining Magistrate was roused to fresh indignation.

"I presume he is more qualified to recognize a demented person on the street than our worthy policemen grubbing around the town, or than you or me?"

Maigret didn't reply.

It was past midnight.

"Are you sure you wouldn't like to sleep here?"

"My bags are at the hotel."

"Shall I see you tomorrow morning?"

"Of course."

"I'll be at the Palais de Justice. You know where it is?"

"On Rue Rabelais, isn't it?"

"A little farther up than the Vernouxs' house. You'll notice the prison railings first, then a not very imposing building. My office is at the end of the hall, near that of the Public Prosecutor."

"Good night, old man."

"I have welcomed you poorly."

"Of course not!"

"You must understand my state of mind. It's the kind of case that could set the whole town against me."

"Indeed!"

"You're laughing at me?"

"No, I promise you."

This was true. Maigret was sad, rather, as one is each time one sees a little of the past vanish. In the hallway, as he struggled into his sodden overcoat, he sniffed again the smell of the house that had always appeared so pleasant to him and now seemed musty.

Chabot had lost practically all his hair, which left uncovered a pointed cranium, like that of certain birds.

"I'll drive you back. . . ."

He did not really want to. He said it out of politeness.

"Certainly not!"

Maigret added a not very subtle joke, for something to say, to finish on a cheerful note:

"I know how to swim!"

Whereupon, turning up the collar of his coat, he plunged into the storm. Julien Chabot remained for a while in the rectangle of pale yellow light, then the door closed again, and Maigret had the impression that, in the streets of the town, there was no one else still about besides himself.

3

The streets presented a more depressing sight in the light of morning than at night, because the rain had dirtied everything, leaving its dark traces on the façades of buildings, turning their colors ugly. Large drops still fell from cornices and electric wires, occasionally from the sky, which was draining itself, still in a dramatic style, as though gathering strength for fresh convulsions.

Maigret, having risen late, had not felt in the mood to go downstairs for his breakfast. Ill-tempered, with no appetite, he simply wanted two or three cups of black coffee. In spite of Chabot's brandy, he thought he could still discern in his mouth the aftertaste of the oversweet white wine he had consumed in Bordeaux.

He pressed a little pear-shaped bell hanging by the head of his bed. The chambermaid, in black with a white apron, who answered his call, looked at him so strangely that he felt obliged to check that he was decently covered.

"Are you sure you wouldn't like some hot croissants? A man like you needs to eat in the morning."

"Only coffee, my dear. An enormous pot of coffee."

She noticed the suit of clothes the Chief Inspector had put to dry over the radiator the night before, and seized them.

"What are you doing?"

"I'm just going to press them."

"No thank you. It's not worth it."

She took them, just the same!

Judging by her physical appearance, he would have said that she was usually rather a crosspatch.

Twice while he was dressing she came and disturbed him, once to make sure he had some soap, and again to bring a second pot of coffee, which he hadn't ordered. Then she returned with his suit, dry and pressed. She was thin, flat-chested, with a look of having poor health, but was probably as tough as iron.

It crossed his mind that she had seen his name on the register, downstairs, and that she was an avid reader of news items.

It was nine-thirty in the morning. He dawdled, in protest against something or other, something he vaguely considered to be a conspiracy of the fates.

As he descended the red-carpeted staircase, a handyman, coming up, greeted him with a respectful:

"Good morning, Monsieur Maigret."

On arriving in the lobby, he understood, for *Ouest-Eclair* was displayed on a small table, with his photograph on the front page.

It was the picture taken when he was bending over Gobillard's body. A large headline announced across three columns:

CHIEF INSPECTOR MAIGRET ENGAGED ON
THE FONTENAY CRIMES
A RABBITSKIN DEALER THE THIRD VICTIM

Before he had time to glance through the article, the hotel manager came up to him, with as much eagerness as the chambermaid.

"I hope you slept well and that Number 17 didn't disturb you too much?"

"Who's Number 17?"

"A salesman who drank too much last night and was noisy. We eventually put him in another room, so that he wouldn't wake you."

He had heard nothing.

"By the way, Lomel, the *Ouest-Eclair* correspondent, came in to see you this morning. When I told him you were still in bed, he said there was no hurry and that he would see you shortly at the Palais de Justice. There's a letter for you, as well."

A cheap envelope, such as are sold in packs of six, in six different colors, in grocery stores. This one was greenish. Just as he was opening it, Maigret realized that there were half a dozen people outside pressing their faces to the glass door, between the palm trees in tubs.

"Don't let yourself be inflewenced by them that's High Sossiety."

The people waiting on the sidewalk, two of them women dressed to go shopping, drew aside to let him pass, and there was something trusting, friendly in the

45

way they looked at him, not so much out of curiosity, not so much because he was a celebrity, but as if they counted on him. One of the women said, without daring to come nearer:

"You'll find him, Monsieur Maigret, you will!"

And a youngster who looked like a delivery boy kept pace with him on the opposite sidewalk, the better to look at him.

On the doorsteps, women were discussing the latest crime and broke off to watch him go by. A group came out of the Café de la Poste, and there too he read sympathy in their eyes. They seemed to want to encourage him.

He passed Chabot's house, where Rose was shaking a duster out of the second-floor window, didn't stop, crossed Place Viète and ascended Rue Rabelais, where on the left stood a vast town house, a coat of arms emblazoned on the pediment, which must surely be the Vernouxs' mansion. There was no sign of life behind the closed windows. Opposite, a little house, also an old one, with closed shutters, was probably where Robert de Courçon had lived out his solitary days.

From time to time there blew a small gust of damp wind. Clouds were driving low, dark against a sky the color of frosted glass, and drops of water were falling from their fringe. The railings of the prison seemed blacker for being wet. Some ten people were standing about in front of the Palais de Justice, which was not at all imposing, being smaller, in fact, than the Vernouxs' house, but which was nevertheless graced with a row of columns and a low flight of steps.

Lomel, with his two cameras still slung around him, was the first to hurry forward, and there wasn't a trace of remorse on his baby face or in his bright-blue eyes.

"Will you let me have your impressions before you give them to my Paris colleagues?"

And as Maigret scowlingly pointed to the newspaper sticking out of his pocket, he smiled.

"Are you annoyed?"

"I thought I'd told you . . ."

"Listen, Inspector. I have to do my job as a journalist. I knew you would eventually become concerned in the case. I've simply anticipated by a few hours . . ."

"Another time, don't anticipate."

"Are you going to see Magistrate Chabot?"

Among the group there were two or three reporters from Paris already and he had difficulty in getting rid of them. There were also a few inquisitive people who seemed determined to spend the day on guard outside the Palais de Justice.

The hallways were dark. Lomel, his self-appointed guide, went ahead, showing him the way.

"Along here. It's much more important for us than for the rag-mongers in the capital! You must realize that! 'He' has been in his office since eight o'clock this morning. The Public Prosecutor's here too. Last night, when they were looking for him everywhere, he was at La Rochelle, where he'd popped over by car. Do you know the Prosecutor?"

Maigret, who had knocked and been called to enter, opened the door and closed it behind him, leaving the redheaded reporter in the hall.

Julien Chabot was not alone. Dr. Alain Vernoux was sitting opposite him in an armchair and got up to greet the Chief Inspector.

"Did you sleep well?" the Magistrate inquired.

"Not at all badly."

"I've been reproaching myself for my poor hospitality last night. You know Alain Vernoux. He's dropped in to see me."

That wasn't true. Maigret was sure that it was he for whom the psychiatrist was waiting and even, perhaps, that this interview had been arranged between the two men.

Vernoux had taken off his overcoat. He was wearing a suit of rough wool, which with its indeterminate creases, could have done with some pressing. His tie was badly knotted. A yellow sweater protruded from under his vest. His shoes had not been polished. Even like this, he nonetheless belonged to the same class as his father, whose appearance was so meticulous.

Why did it make Maigret wince? One was too well groomed, dressed to the nines. The other, on the contrary, affected a carelessness that a bank employee, a schoolmaster, or a salesman could not have allowed himself; yet, one surely did not find suits of such material except at an exclusive tailor's in Paris, or possibly Bordeaux.

There was a rather embarrassing silence. Maigret, who was doing nothing to help the two men, went and stood in front of the meager log fire beneath the mantelpiece, which was surmounted by the same black marble clock as the one in his own office at Quai des Orfèvres. At some time the authorities must have ordered them in hundreds, if not thousands. Perhaps they all alike lost twelve minutes a day, like Maigret's?

"Alain was just telling me some interesting things," murmured Chabot at last, his chin in his hand, in a pose very much that of an examining magistrate. "We were speaking of criminal lunacy . . ."

Vernoux's son interrupted him.

"I haven't asserted that these three crimes are the work of a lunatic. I said that, *if they were the work of a lunatic* . . ."

"That comes to the same thing."

"Not exactly."

"Let's put it that it's I who said everything seems to indicate that we are confronted by a lunatic."

And, turning to Maigret:

"We talked about this yesterday evening, you and I. The absence of motive in the three cases . . . The similarity of method . . ."

Then, to Vernoux:

"So, will you repeat to the Chief Inspector what you were explaining to me?"

"I'm not an expert. In these matters I am only an amateur. I was developing a general idea. Most people suppose that lunatics invariably act like lunatics, that is to say, without logic or continuity of ideas. Now, in reality, it is often the contrary. Lunatics have their own logic. The difficulty lies in detecting that logic."

Maigret was looking at him, with his large eyes slightly sea green in the morning light, without saying anything. He was sorry he hadn't stopped on the way to have a drink, which would have put new life in his belly.

This small office, where a layer of smoke from his pipe was beginning to float and the little flames from the logs were dancing, seemed scarcely real to him, and the two men discussing madness, watching him out of the corners of their eyes, appeared to him rather like wax figures. They too formed no part of real life. They were making gestures they had learned, speaking as they had been taught to.

What could a man like Chabot know of what went on in the street? And, still more so, in the mind of a killer?

"It is that logic, since the first crime, I have been trying to penetrate."

"Since the first crime?"

"Let's say, since the second. From the first, however, from the murder of my uncle, I thought it was the act of a madman."

"Have you found anything out?"

"Not yet. I've only noted a few elements of the problem, which might provide a clue."

"Such as?"

"Such as, that he strikes from the front. It's not easy to express my idea simply. A man who wanted to kill in order to kill, that is to say, to do away with other living beings, and who at the same time wouldn't like to be caught, would choose the least dangerous method. Now, this one certainly doesn't want to get caught, because he avoids leaving any traces. Do you follow me?"

"It's not too complicated, up to now."

Vernoux frowned, sensing the irony in Maigret's voice. It was possible that, fundamentally, he lacked confidence. He did not look people in the eye. From the shelter of the large lenses of his glasses, he merely gave furtive little glances, then gazed at some point in space.

"You admit that he'll do anything rather than be caught?"

"It looks like it."

"Nevertheless, he attacks three people in the same week, and all three times he brings it off."

"True."

"In all three cases, he might have struck from behind,

which would have reduced the chances of a victim starting to call out."

Maigret stared hard at him.

"Because even a madman does nothing without reason, I deduce from this that the murderer feels the need to fly in the face of fate, or in the face of those whom he assaults. Certain characters need to assert themselves, whether by one crime or by a series of crimes. Sometimes, it's in order to prove their power, or their importance, or their courage to themselves. Others are convinced they have to avenge themselves on their fellow men."

"This one, up to now, has only attacked the weak. Robert de Courçon was an old man of seventy-three. The widow Gibon was a cripple, and Gobillard, at the time he was assaulted, was dead drunk."

It was the Magistrate this time who had spoken, his chin still in his hand, evidently pleased with himself.

"I thought of that too. Perhaps it's a clue, perhaps it's a coincidence. What I'm trying to discover is the sort of logic that directs the actions and conduct of this unknown person. When we have discovered that, it won't be long before we get our hands on him."

He said "we" as if he were participating in the investigation as a matter of course, and Chabot didn't object.

"Was it for that reason you were out last night?" inquired the Chief Inspector.

Alain Vernoux started, blushed slightly.

"Partly. I was actually calling on a friend, but I do admit to you that, for the last three days, I have been going about the streets as often as possible, studying the behavior of the passers-by. The town isn't large. It's more than likely the murderer isn't hiding out at home. He is around on the sidewalks, like everyone else, maybe having a drink in the cafés."

"Do you think you would recognize him if you met him?"

"I think that Alain may be invaluable to us," Chabot murmured with a touch of embarrassment. "What he has said to us this morning seems to me full of good sense."

The doctor rose, and at the same time a noise was heard in the hall. Someone knocked at the door, and Inspector Chabiron put his head in.

"You're not alone?" he said, looking, not at Maigret, but at Alain Vernoux, whose presence appeared to displease him.

"What is it, Inspector?"

"I have someone with me I would like you to question."

The doctor announced:

"I will go."

Nobody stopped him. As he was going out, Chabiron said to Maigret, not without some bitterness:

"So it seems you're taking a hand, Chief?"

"The newspaper says so."

"Perhaps the case won't take long. It might be all over in a couple of minutes. Shall I bring my witness in, Magistrate?"

And, turning to the half-darkness of the hall:

"Come on! Don't be afraid."

A voice replied:

"I'm not afraid."

They saw a small, thin man enter, dressed in navy blue, with a pale face, eager eyes.

Chabiron introduced him:

"Emile Chalus, schoolmaster at the boys' school. Sit down, Chalus."

Chabiron was one of those policemen who invariably used "*tu*" to both offenders and witnesses in the belief that it would impress them.

"Last night," he explained, "I began interrogating people living on the street where Gobillard was killed. You may say, perhaps, it's just routine . . ."

He threw a glance at Maigret, as if the Chief Inspector were a personal enemy of routine.

". . . but sometimes routine produces results. The street is not a long one. Early this morning I went on combing the area minutely. Emile Chalus lives thirty yards from the spot where the crime was committed, on the third floor of a house that has offices on the first and second floors. Tell them your story, Chalus."

The latter was longing to say his piece, in spite of the fact that he obviously had no sympathy for the Magistrate. It was to Maigret that he turned.

"I heard a noise like the sound of feet on the sidewalk."

"At what time?"

"A little after ten in the evening."

"And then?"

"The footsteps went away."

"In which direction?"

The Examining Magistrate was asking the questions, each time looking at Maigret as though to offer him the chance to speak.

"In the direction of Rue de la République."

"Hurried footsteps?"

"No. Normal steps."

"A man's?"

"Definitely."

Chabot looked as though he thought it was not a very startling revelation, but the Inspector intervened.

"Wait for the rest. Tell them what happened afterward, Chalus."

"A few minutes went by and then a group of people came into the street, coming from Rue de la République too. They gathered together on the sidewalk, talking loudly. I heard the word 'doctor,' then the words 'police inspector,' and I got up to look out the window."

Chabiron was gloating.

"Do you understand, Magistrate? Chalus also heard running footsteps. Just now he informed me that there had also been a muffled noise, like that of a body falling on the sidewalk. Repeat what you said, Chalus."

"That is correct."

"Immediately after, someone went off in the direction of Rue de la République, where the Café de la Poste is. I have other witnesses waiting outside, customers who were in the café at that time. It was ten past ten when Doctor Vernoux went in there, without saying anything, and went straight to the telephone booth. After he had telephoned, he noticed Doctor Jussieux playing cards, and whispered something in his ear. Jussieux announced to the others that a crime had just been committed and they all rushed outside."

Maigret gazed at his friend Chabot, whose expression had stiffened.

"You see what that means?" the Inspector went on, with a kind of aggressive delight, as though he were taking a personal revenge. "According to Doctor Vernoux, he found a body on the sidewalk, a body already almost cold, and he went off to the Café de la Poste in order to telephone the police. If this were so, there would have been two sounds of footsteps in the street, and Chalus, who wasn't asleep, would have heard them."

He didn't yet dare to exult, but they could sense his excitement growing.

"Chalus has no criminal record. He's a respectable schoolmaster. He has no motive for inventing a story."

Maigret refused once again the invitation to speak, which his friend offered him with a glance. There followed quite a long pause. To hide his feelings, probably, the Magistrate scribbled a few words in a file he had in front of him, and when he raised his head again, he was looking tense.

"Are you married, Monsieur Chalus?" he asked in a dull voice.

"Yes, sir."

The hostility between the two men was palpable. Chalus was tense too, and his manner of replying aggressive. He seemed to be challenging the Magistrate to destroy his evidence.

"Any children?"

"No."

"Was your wife with you last night?"

"In the same bed."

"She was asleep?"

"Yes."

"You went to bed at the same time?"

"As usual, when I haven't too much homework to correct. Yesterday was Friday and I had none at all."

"At what time did you and your wife go to bed?"

"Half past nine, perhaps a few minutes later."

"Do you always go to bed so early?"

"We get up at half past five in the morning."

"Why?"

"Because we make use of the freedom that is accorded to all French people to get up at whatever hour they please."

Maigret, who was watching him with interest, felt pretty certain that he was active in politics, belonged to a left-wing party, and was probably what is called "militant." He was the kind of man to march in processions, to speak at meetings, the kind of man also to slip pamphlets in mailboxes and refuse to move on, in spite of injunctions from the police.

"So you were both in bed at half past nine, and I presume you fell asleep?"

"We went on talking for about ten minutes."

"That takes us to twenty to ten. You both fell asleep?"

"My wife went to sleep."

"And you?"

"No. I find it difficult to get to sleep."

"So that, when you heard the noise on the sidewalk, thirty yards from your house, you were not asleep."

"That is correct."

"You hadn't been to sleep at all?"

"No."

"You were wide awake?"

"Enough to hear running footsteps and the noise of a body falling."

"Was it raining?"

"Yes."

"There isn't a floor above yours?"

"No. We are on the top."

"You must have heard the rain on the roof?"

"You don't notice it after a bit."

"Water running down the gutter?"

"Certainly."

"So that the sounds you heard were just sounds among other sounds?"

"There is an appreciable difference between running water and the trample of men's feet or a body falling."

The Magistrate was not giving up yet.

"You hadn't the curiosity to get up?"

"No."

"Why not?"

"Because we aren't far from the Café de la Poste."

"I don't understand."

"Frequently, at night, men who have drunk too much pass our house, and sometimes they collapse on the sidewalk."

"And stay there too?"

Chalus could find nothing to answer to that right away.

"Since you have spoken of running feet, I presume you got the impression that there were several men in the street, at least two anyway?"

"That goes without saying."

"Only one man disappeared in the direction of Rue de la République. Is that right?"

"I suppose so."

"Since there was a crime, two men at the very least were thirty yards from your house, at the time you heard running footsteps. Do you follow me?"

"It's not difficult."

"You heard one going off again?"

"I've already said so."

"When did you hear them arrive? Did they arrive

57

together? Did they come from Rue de la République or from the Champ de Mars?"

Chabiron shrugged his shoulders. Emile Chalus was pondering, with a stern expression.

"I didn't hear them arrive."

"You don't suppose, however, that they had been standing in the rain for a long time, one of them awaiting a propitious moment to kill the other?"

The schoolmaster clenched his fists.

"Is that all you've got out of it?" he muttered between his teeth.

"I don't understand."

"It embarrasses you that someone from your own circle may be involved. But your question is ridiculous. I don't necessarily hear someone walking along the sidewalk, or, rather, I don't pay particular attention to it."

"However . . ."

"Let me finish, will you, instead of trying to trap me. Up to the time of the running footsteps, I had no reason to pay any attention to what was happening in the street. Afterward, on the other hand, my mind was alert."

"And you maintain that from the time the body fell on the sidewalk until the time when several people arrived from the Café de la Poste, not a soul passed along the street?"

"There wasn't a single footstep."

"Do you realize the importance of this statement?"

"I didn't ask to make it. It was the Inspector who came to question me."

"Before the Inspector questioned you, you hadn't the slightest idea of the significance of what you had noticed?"

"I was unaware of Doctor Vernoux's testimony."

58

"Who has told you about any testimony? Doctor Vernoux hasn't been called to testify."

"Let's say that I was unaware of his story."

"Was it the Inspector who told you?"

"Yes."

"Then you realized?"

"Yes."

"And I suppose you were delighted with the effect you were going to produce? You hate the Vernouxs?"

"Them, and all like them."

"Have you specifically attacked them in your speeches?"

"It has happened."

The Magistrate, very frigid, turned to Inspector Chabiron.

"Has his wife confirmed what he says?"

"Partly. I didn't bring her because she was busy in the house, but I can go and fetch her. They certainly went to bed at half past nine. She is sure of this because it is she who winds the alarm clock each evening. They talked for a little while. She went to sleep, and was waked up again by finding that her husband was no longer beside her. She saw him standing at the window. At that time, it was a quarter past ten, and a group of people were standing around the corpse."

"Did neither of them go downstairs?"

"No."

"They weren't curious to know what was happening?"

"They opened the window a little, and heard someone saying that Gobillard had just been murdered."

Chabot, who still avoided Maigret's eyes, seemed discouraged. Without conviction, he asked yet a few more questions:

"Do any other people living on the street support his evidence?"

"Not so far."

"Have you questioned them all?"

"Those who were at home this morning. Some had already gone off to work. Two or three others, who were at the movies last night, know nothing."

Chabot turned to the schoolmaster.

"Do you know Doctor Vernoux personally?"

"I've never spoken to him, if that's what you mean. I've passed him in the street often enough, like everyone else. I know who he is."

"You don't have any particular animosity against him?"

"I have already replied to that."

"Have you ever appeared in court?"

"I've been arrested a good dozen times, in political demonstrations, but after a night in jail and the usual rough handling, they have always let me out."

"I am not concerned with that."

"I realize that it doesn't interest you."

"Do you stick to your statement?"

"Yes, even if it upsets you."

"It doesn't affect me."

"It affects your friends."

"Are you so sure of what you heard yesterday evening that you wouldn't hesitate to send someone to prison or to the scaffold?"

"I haven't done any killing. The murderer himself didn't hesitate to do away with the widow Gibon and poor Gobillard."

"You are forgetting Robert de Courçon."

"About him, I couldn't care a f . . . !"

"Well, I shall call the clerk of the court so that he can take down your statement in writing."

"I'm at your disposal."

"Then we shall hear your wife's evidence."

"She won't contradict me."

Chabot was already reaching out his hand toward an electric bell on his desk when the voice of Maigret, who had almost been forgotten, asked quietly:

"Do you suffer from insomnia, Monsieur Chalus?"

The latter quickly turned his head.

"What are you trying to insinuate?"

"Nothing. I believe I heard you say, just now, that you find it hard to get to sleep, which explains why, though you were in bed by half past nine, you were still awake at ten o'clock."

"For some years now I've had insomnia."

"Have you consulted a doctor?"

"I don't like doctors."

"Haven't you tried any remedy?"

"I take some pills."

"Every day?"

"Is it a crime?"

"Did you take some yesterday before going to bed?"

"I took two of them, as I generally do."

Maigret nearly smiled, seeing his friend Chabot revive, like a plant long deprived of moisture which has been watered at last. The Magistrate couldn't resist resuming the direction of operations himself.

"Why didn't you tell us you had taken a sleeping pill?"

"Because you didn't ask me and because it's my affair. Should I also tell you when my wife takes a purgative?"

"You swallowed two pills at half past nine?"

"Yes."

"And you weren't asleep by ten past ten?"

"No. If you were in the habit of taking such drugs, you would know that in the end they have almost no effect. To start with, one pill was enough for me. Now, with two, it takes me more than half an hour to feel drowsy."

"It's possible, then, that when you heard the noise in the street, you were already drowsy?"

"I wasn't asleep. If I had been asleep, I should have heard nothing."

"But you could have been dozing. What were you thinking about?"

"I don't remember."

"Can you swear you were not in a state between waking and sleeping? Consider my question seriously. Perjury is a grave offense."

"I was not asleep."

The man was basically honest. He had certainly been delighted to be able to bring down a member of the Vernoux clan and he had done it with glee. Now feeling the triumph slip through his fingers, he was trying to cling to it, without quite daring to lie.

He cast Maigret an unhappy look tinged with reproach but not anger. He seemed to be saying:

"Why have you let me down, when you aren't on their side?"

The Magistrate wasted no time.

"Suppose that the pills had begun to take effect without, however, putting you to sleep completely; it may be that you did hear the noises in the street, and your drowsiness would explain why you had not heard any footsteps before the murder. It needed a scuffle of feet, the fall of a body, to attract your attention. Isn't it plausible that immediately after the footsteps died away, you fell again into a drowsy state? You didn't get up. You didn't wake your wife. You weren't worried—you told us so yourself—as if the whole thing had happened in another world. It wasn't until several men, talking in loud voices, stopped on the sidewalk that you were completely roused."

Chalus shrugged his shoulders and let them fall again wearily.

"I might have expected this," he said.

Then he added something like:

"You and your type . . ."

Chabot wasn't listening any more; he was saying to Inspector Chabiron:

"You can still draw up a report of his statement. I will hear his wife this afternoon."

When he and Maigret were alone, the Magistrate made a show of taking some notes. A good five minutes went by before he murmured, without looking at the Chief Inspector:

"Thank you."

And Maigret, sucking his pipe:

"There's nothing to thank me for."

4

Throughout the entire luncheon, the main course of which was a stuffed shoulder of mutton, the like of which Maigret could not remember ever having eaten, Julien Chabot had the air of a man suffering from a bad conscience.

As they had entered the front door of his house, he had felt it necessary to mutter:

"We mustn't mention any of this in front of my mother."

Maigret had had no intention of doing so. He noticed that his friend bent down to the mailbox, from which, discarding a few circulars, he took an envelope similar to the one he had been handed that morning in the hotel, with the difference that this one, instead of being pale green, was salmon pink. Perhaps it had come from the same pack? He wasn't able to make sure just then, since the Magistrate slipped it carelessly into his pocket.

They had hardly spoken a word while returning from the Palais de Justice. Before leaving there, they had had a short interview with the Public Prosecutor, and Maigret had been considerably surprised to find that he was a man barely thirty years old, hardly out of school, a handsome fellow who did not seem to take his duties too seriously.

"I'm sorry about last night, Chabot. There's a good reason why they didn't manage to get hold of me. I was at La Rochelle and my wife didn't know about it."

He added with a wink:

"Fortunately!"

Then, suspecting nothing:

"Now that you have Chief Inspector Maigret to help you, it won't be long before you catch the murderer. Do you also think he's a lunatic, Chief Inspector?"

What use was there in discussing it? You could tell that relations between the Examining Magistrate and the Public Prosecutor were not overfriendly.

In the hallway there was the onslaught of journalists, who already had wind of Chalus's evidence. The latter had probably talked to them. Maigret would have wagered that it was known about all over the town too. It was difficult to explain the atmosphere here. From the Palais de Justice to the Magistrate's house they saw only about fifty people, but it was enough to take the local pulse. The looks the two men received showed a lack of confidence. The working-class people, particularly women returning from shopping, had an almost hostile attitude.

At the top of Place Viète there was a little café where

quite a number of people were taking their apéritifs, and, as they passed it, they heard a somewhat disturbing buzz of talk and derisive laughter.

Some people were probably starting to panic, and the presence of policemen patrolling the town on bicycles was not sufficient to reassure them; on the contrary, they added a touch of drama to the appearance of the streets, by reminding people that somewhere about there was a murderer at large.

Madame Chabot had not attempted to ask questions. She was full of little attentions to her son, to Maigret too, whom she seemed to be asking, from her expression, to protect him, and she was doing her best to introduce perfectly innocuous subjects into the conversation.

"Do you remember the young girl with a squint with whom you had dinner here one Sunday?"

She had a terrifying memory, reminding Maigret of people he had met more than thirty years before, during his visits to Fontenay.

"She made a fine marriage, a young man from Marans who started a successful cheese business. They had three children, each more beautiful than the last. Then all of a sudden, as if fate had decided they were too happy, she was struck down by tuberculosis."

She mentioned others who had become invalids or had died, or had suffered similar misfortunes.

For dessert, Rose brought in an enormous dish of profiteroles, and the old woman watched the Chief Inspector mischievously. He wondered at first why, feeling that something was expected of him. He didn't care very much for profiteroles and he put one of them on his plate.

"Go on! Help yourself. Don't be ashamed! . . ."

Seeing she was disappointed, he took three.

"Don't tell me you've lost your liking for them! I remember the evening you ate twelve. Each time you came
I made profiteroles for you, and you used to maintain
that you'd never eaten such good ones anywhere else."

(Which was, incidentally, true: he never ate them at all
anywhere else!)

It had all passed out of his memory. He was even surprised that he had ever shown a taste for pastries. He
must have said so, once, for politeness' sake.

He did his duty, exclaimed his appreciation, ate all he
had on his plate, took some more.

"And the partridge with cabbage! Do you remember
that? I am sorry it's the wrong season now, for . . ."

When coffee was served, she withdrew discreetly, and
Chabot, as was his custom, placed a box of cigars on the
table, together with a bottle of brandy. The dining room
was as little altered as the study, and it was almost painful
to find things so much the same, including Chabot himself, who, in some ways, hadn't altered much either.

To please his friend, Maigret took a cigar, stretched his
legs out toward the hearth. He knew that the other man
wanted to broach a particular subject, that he had been
thinking about it ever since they had left the Palais. It
took time. The Magistrate's voice, as he looked the other
way, lacked confidence.

"You think I should have arrested him?"

"Who?"

"Alain."

"I see no reason for arresting the doctor."

"Yet Chalus seemed sincere."

"He's that, undeniably."

"You too think he wasn't telling lies."

Deep down, Chabot was wondering why Maigret had

intervened, because but for him, but for the point about the sleeping pills, the schoolmaster's statement would have been much more damaging for the younger Vernoux. It perplexed the Magistrate, made him ill at ease.

"First of all," said Maigret, smoking his cigar awkwardly, "it's possible that he really had dozed off. I always mistrust the evidence of people who have heard something from their beds, perhaps because of my wife.

"Time and again she insists that she hasn't got to sleep until two o'clock in the morning. She says it in all good faith, ready to swear to it. Now, quite often, I've waked up myself during her so-called insomnia and I've seen her asleep."

Chabot wasn't convinced. Perhaps he imagined that his friend had simply wanted to save him from an awkward situation?

"Furthermore," continued the Chief Inspector, "even if the doctor is the murderer, it's better he should not be put under arrest yet. He's not the sort of man from whom one can extort a confession through plain interrogation, still less through any rough handling."

The Magistrate was already rejecting this idea with an indignant gesture.

"In the present state of the investigations there isn't even a particle of proof against him. By arresting him, you would give satisfaction to a section of the population who would come and demonstrate under the prison windows, shouting: 'Kill him.' Once such a disturbance began, it would be difficult to suppress it."

"Do you really think so?"

"Yes."

"You aren't saying so in order to reassure me?"

"I say so because it's the truth. As always happens in a case of this kind, public opinion points pretty frankly to one suspect or another, and I've often wondered how it chooses him. It's a mysterious phenomenon, rather a frightening one. From the first day, if I'm not mistaken, the people have turned against the Vernoux family, without caring too much whether it's the father or the son."

"That's true."

"Now it's on the son that they're venting their anger."

"And supposing he is the murderer?"

"I heard you, before leaving, giving orders for him to be watched."

"He may escape his watchers."

"It wouldn't be wise of him to do so, because if he shows himself much in the town, he runs the risk of being torn to pieces. If it is he, he will do something sooner or later that will give us a clue."

"Perhaps you are right. I really am glad that you're here. Yesterday, I admit, it bothered me a little, I told myself you would be watching me and that you'd find me clumsy, awkward, old-fashioned, and I don't know what else. In the provinces, we almost all suffer from an inferiority complex, especially in the face of people from Paris. Even more so when it's a man like you! Do you blame me?"

"For what?"

"For the stupid things I've been saying."

"You've said some very sensible things. In Paris, we too have to take into account different situations and put ourselves in other people's shoes."

Chabot already felt better.

"I shall spend my afternoon interrogating the witnesses Chabiron has hunted up for me. Most of them have neither seen nor heard anything, but I don't want to miss any chance."

"Be nice to Chalus's wife."

"Yes, certainly! . . . Will you come with me?"

"No. I'd rather scout around the town, drink a glass of beer here and there."

"Well now, I haven't opened this letter. I didn't want to do so in front of my mother."

He took the salmon-colored envelope from his pocket, and Maigret recognized the handwriting. The paper definitely came from the same pack as the note he had received that morning.

"Find out what the doctor was doing at the Sabati girl's."

"Do you know?"

"Never heard that name."

"I think I remember you told me that Doctor Vernoux doesn't run after girls."

"He's reputed not to. Anonymous letters are going to pour in now. This one comes from a woman."

"As most anonymous letters do! Would you mind phoning the police station?"

"About the Sabati girl?"

"Yes."

"Right away?"

Maigret nodded.

"Let's go into my study."

He lifted the receiver, called the police station.

"Is that you, Féron? The Examining Magistrate speaking. Do you know a woman named Sabati?"

They had to wait. Féron had gone to ask his men, perhaps to examine the files. When he came on the line again, Chabot took down a few words in pencil on his blotter while he listened.

"No. Probably no connection. . . . What? . . . Certainly not. Don't do anything about her for the moment."

In saying this, he looked for Maigret's approval and the latter nodded his head vigorously.

"I'll be in my office in half an hour. Yes. Thank you."

He hung up.

"There is indeed a certain Louise Sabati in Fontenay-le-Comte. Daughter of an Italian builder who's supposed to be working in Nantes or thereabouts. For some time she was a waitress at the Hôtel de France, then a barmaid at the Café de la Poste. She hasn't worked for several months. Unless she's moved recently, she lives on the bend in the La Rochelle road near the barracks, in a large dilapidated house with six or seven families living in it."

Maigret, who had had enough of his cigar, crushed out the glowing stub in the ashtray, before filling a pipe.

"Are you thinking of going to see her?"

"Perhaps."

"You still think that the doctor . . . ?"

He stopped short, his eyebrows puckered.

"Well, what shall we do this evening? Normally I would be going to the Vernouxs' for bridge. From what you've told me, Hubert Vernoux is expecting you to come with me."

"Well?"

"I'm wondering whether, in the present climate of opinion . . ."

"Are you in the habit of going there every Saturday?"

"Yes."

"In that case, if you don't go, people will conclude that they're under suspicion."

"And if I do go, they'll say . . ."

"They'll say you're protecting them, that's all. They're saying so already. One way or another . . ."

"Do you intend to come with me?"

"Without the slightest hesitation."

"All right then . . ."

Poor Chabot had given up resisting, left all the initiative to Maigret. "It's time I went up to the Palais."

They went out together, and the sky had still the same whiteness, at once bright and blue-green, the kind of sky one sees reflected in the water of a pool. The wind was still fierce and, at street corners, women's dresses clung to their bodies; sometimes a man would lose his hat and have to run after it, waving his arms grotesquely.

They were going off in opposite directions.

"When shall I see you again?"

"I may call in at your chambers. If not, I'll be at your house for dinner. What time is bridge at the Vernouxs'?"

"Half past eight."

"I warn you I don't know how to play."

"It doesn't matter."

Curtains moved as Maigret passed along the sidewalk, his pipe between his teeth, his hands in his pockets, his head bent to prevent his hat from flying off. Now he was on his own, he felt a little less confident. All that he had just said to his friend Chabot was true. But when he had intervened, that morning, at the end of Chalus's interrogation, although he had acted on impulse, there was still, at the back of it, the desire to rescue the Magistrate from an embarrassing situation.

The atmosphere of the town remained disquieting. Even though people had gone to work as usual, one sensed nonetheless a certain anxiety in the looks of the passers-by, who seemed to be walking more quickly, as if they expected to see the murderer suddenly spring out. On other days, Maigret felt sure, the housewives would not have gathered in groups on doorsteps as they did today, talking in low voices.

Their eyes followed him, and he thought he could read a silent question in their faces. Was he going to do something? Or would the unknown person be able to go on killing with impunity?

Some of them addressed him with a timid greeting, as if to say:

"We know who you are. You have a reputation for solving the most difficult cases. And *you* won't let yourself be impressed by certain individuals."

He almost entered the Café de la Poste to drink a half-pint. Unfortunately, there were at least a dozen people inside whose heads all turned toward him when he approached the door, and suddenly he had no desire to have to reply to the questions they would put to him.

Finally, in order to reach the barracks district, he had to cross the Champ de Mars, a vast bare expanse bordered by trees recently planted, which were shaking in the icy wind.

He took the same little street the doctor had taken the evening before, the one in which Gobillard had been struck down. As he passed one house, he heard the sound of angry voices on the top floor. It was doubtless where Emile Chalus, the schoolmaster, lived. Several people were arguing passionately, some of his friends who had probably come for news.

He crossed the Champ de Mars, skirted the barracks, took the street to the right, and looked for the large dilapidated building his friend had described to him. There was only one of this type, in a deserted street, between two empty lots. What it had formerly been was hard to tell—a warehouse or a mill, perhaps a small factory? Some children were playing outside. Others, younger ones, with bare bottoms, were crawling about in the hallway. A fat woman with hair falling down her back put her head around the narrow opening of a door, and she had never before heard the name of Chief Inspector Maigret.

"Who are you looking for?"

"Mademoiselle Sabati."

"Louise?"

"I think that's her Christian name."

"Go right around the house and in by the door at the back. Go up the stairs. There's only one door. That's it."

He did what he was told, brushed past garbage cans, stepped over trash, and all the time he could hear the bugles sounding in the barracks square. The outside door he had just been told about was open. A steep staircase, without a banister, led him to a floor that wasn't on the same level as the rest, and he knocked on a blue-painted door.

At first, no one answered. He knocked louder, heard the footsteps of a woman in slippers, yet had to knock still a third time before he was asked:

"What is it?"

"Mademoiselle Sabati?"

"What do you want?"

"To talk to you."

He added on the off chance:

"The doctor sent me."

"One moment."

She went off again, probably to slip on some suitable

garment. When she at last opened the door, she was wearing a flowered dressing gown, of cheap cotton, under which she probably had on only a nightdress. Her feet were bare in her slippers, her black hair uncombed.

"Were you asleep?"

"No."

She studied him from head to foot with mistrust. Behind her, beyond a diminutive landing, could be seen an untidy room, which she didn't invite him to enter.

"What does *he* want me to say."

As she turned her head slightly to one side, he noticed a bruise around her left eye. It wasn't altogether a fresh one. It was beginning to turn from blue to yellow.

"Don't be afraid. I'm a friend. I'd just like to talk to you for a few minutes."

What probably decided her to let him enter was the fact that two or three children had come to look at them from the bottom of the stairs.

There were only two rooms, the bedroom, of which he caught only a glimpse and where the bed was unmade, and a kitchen. On the table, a novel was open beside a mug still containing some coffee; a lump of butter was left on a plate.

Louise Sabati was not beautiful. In a black dress and white apron, she must have had that tired look one notices in most chambermaids in provincial hotels. There was, however, something appealing, almost pathetic, in her pale face, where her dark eyes were intensely alive.

She cleared things off a chair.

"Did Alain really send you?"

"No."

"He doesn't know you're here?"

As she said this she glanced with an utterly terrified

look at the door, and remained standing, on the defensive.

"Don't be afraid."

"You're from the police."

"Yes and no."

"What's happened? Where is Alain?"

"At his home, probably."

"You're sure?"

"Why should he be anywhere else?"

She bit her lip and the blood rose to it. She was very tense, with an unhealthy nervousness. He wondered for a moment if she took drugs.

"Who told you about me?"

"Have you been the doctor's mistress for long?"

"Have they told you that?"

He put on his most affable air, and anyway, he didn't have to make an effort to show sympathy to her.

"You've only just got up?" he asked, instead of replying.

"What business is that of yours?"

She had retained a trace of an Italian accent, no more. She was probably little more than twenty, and her body, under her badly cut dressing gown, was well built; only her bosom, which must once have been provocative, sagged a little.

"Would you mind sitting down beside me?"

She couldn't keep still. With feverish movements, she seized a cigarette, lit it.

"Are you sure Alain won't come?"

"Does it frighten you? Why?"

"He's jealous."

"He hasn't any reason to be jealous of me."

"He is of any man."

She added in an odd voice:

"He's right."

"What do you mean?"

"He's entitled to be."

"He's in love with you?"

"I think so. I know I'm not worth it, but . . ."

"Won't you really sit down?"

"Who are you?"

"Chief Inspector Maigret, from Police Headquarters, Paris."

"I've heard of you. What are you doing here?"

Why not speak frankly to her?

"I happened to come here to meet a friend I hadn't seen for years."

"Was it he who told you about me?"

"No. I've also met your friend Alain. In fact, I've been invited to his house tonight."

She sensed that he wasn't lying, but still wasn't reassured. She nonetheless drew a chair toward her, but didn't sit down right away.

"If he's not in trouble at the moment, he may well be any time now."

"Why?"

From the tone in which she uttered the word, he concluded that she already knew.

"Some people think he may be the man they're looking for."

"Because of the crimes? It's not true. It's not him. He hadn't any reason to . . ."

He interrupted her by handing her the anonymous letter the Magistrate had left with him. She read it, her face tense, frowning.

"I wonder who wrote that."

"A woman."

"Yes. And it must be a woman who lives in this house."

"Why?"

"Because nobody else knows. Even in this house, I could have sworn nobody knew who he is. It's spite, a dirty trick. Alain never . . ."

"Sit down."

She decided at last to do so, taking care to cross the folds of her gown over her bare legs.

"Have you been his mistress long?"

She didn't hesitate.

"Eight months and one week."

This exactness almost made him smile.

"How did it start?"

"I was working as a barmaid in the Café de la Poste. He used to come there from time to time, in the afternoons, always sat in the same place, near the window, where he could look at the people passing. Everyone knew him and greeted him, but he didn't easily open a conversation. After a while, I noticed he was watching me."

She looked at him suddenly, defiantly.

"Do you really want to know how it began? All right, I'll tell you, and you'll see he's not the kind of man you think. Finally he used to come for a drink in the evenings. Once he stayed right up to closing time. I was rather inclined to make fun of him because of his big eyes following me everywhere. That night, I had a date, outside, with the wine merchant, whom you'll certainly meet. We turned right, down the little street, and . . ."

"And what?"

"Oh, well! We settled down on a bench in the Champ de Mars. You understand? That sort of thing never lasted very long. When it was all over, I set off alone to cross the square and return home and I heard steps behind me. It was the doctor. I was a bit scared. I turned around and asked him what he wanted me for. Looking quite shame-faced, he didn't know what to reply. Do you know what he managed to murmur in the end?

" *'Why did you do that?'*

"And I burst out laughing.

" *'Does it upset you?'*

" *'It distressed me a great deal.'*

" *'Why?'*

"That's how, at last, he admitted he loved me, that he'd never dared to tell me, that he was very unhappy. You're smiling?"

"No."

It was true. Maigret was not smiling. He could very well see Alain Vernoux in such a situation.

"We walked about until one or two in the morning, right along the towpath, and, in the end, I was the one who was crying."

"Did he accompany you here?"

"Not that night. It took a whole week. During those days, he spent almost all his time in the café, watching me. He was even jealous seeing me thank a customer when I received a tip. He's like that all the time. He doesn't like me to go out."

"Does he hit you?"

She put her hand instinctively to the bruise on her cheek and, as the sleeve of her dressing gown slipped down, he saw there were other blue marks, on her arms, as if they had been gripped hard between powerful fingers.

"He's entitled to do so," she retorted, not without pride.

79

"Does it often happen?"

"Almost every time."

"Why?"

"If you don't understand, I can't explain it to you. He loves me. He's obliged to live over there with his wife and children. Not only does he not love his wife, but he doesn't like his children either."

"Has he told you so?"

"I know."

"Are you unfaithful to him?"

She shut up, stared at him with a ferocious look. Then:

"Has someone told you so?"

And in a lower voice:

"It did happen, to start with, when I hadn't yet realized. I thought he would be like all the rest. When you've begun, like me, at fourteen, you don't attach any importance to it. When he found out, I thought he was going to kill me. I really mean it. I've never seen a man so terrifying. For a whole hour, he lay stretched out on the bed, his eyes fixed on the ceiling, his fists clenched, without uttering a word, and I could tell he was suffering terribly."

"Did you do it again?"

"Two or three times. I've been pretty stupid."

"And since?"

"No!"

"Does he come to see you every evening?"

"Almost every evening."

"Were you expecting him yesterday?"

She hesitated, wondering what her replies might involve him in, wanting at all costs to protect Alain.

"What difference can it make?"

"You must have gone out to do your shopping."

"I don't go right into town. There's a little grocer on the corner of the street."

"For the rest of the time, you're locked up here?"

"I'm not locked up. You know as much, because I opened the door to you."

"He's never talked of locking you up?"

"How did you guess?"

"He has done so?"

"For one week."

"Did the neighbors realize?"

"Yes."

"That's why he gave you back the key?"

"I don't know. I don't understand what you're getting at."

"Do you love him?"

"Do you suppose I would live this sort of life if I didn't love him?"

"He gives you money?"

"When he can."

"I thought he was rich."

"Everybody thinks that, whereas he's in exactly the same position as a young man who has to ask for a little money from his father every week. They all live in the same house."

"Why?"

"How should I know?"

"He could work."

"That's his business, isn't it? For weeks on end, his father leaves him without money."

Maigret looked at the table, where there was only some bread and some butter.

"Is that the position at the moment?"

She shrugged her shoulders.

"What difference does it make? I too, at one time, used to have notions about people who are supposed to be rich. It's all on the outside! A large house with nothing indoors. They're always squabbling to squeeze a bit of money out of the old man, and the shopkeepers sometimes wait months to get paid."

"I thought Alain's wife was rich."

"If she had been rich, she wouldn't have married him. She imagined that he was. When she found out to the contrary, she began to hate him."

There was a fairly long silence. Maigret filled his pipe, slowly, dreamily.

"What are you busy thinking now?" she asked.

"I'm thinking that you really love him."

"You've got there already!"

Her irony was bitter.

"What I'm wondering," she continued, "is why all at once people are against him. I've read the newspaper. It doesn't say anything definite, but I feel they're suspecting him. Just now, at the window, I heard some women talking in the yard, very loud, on purpose, so that I wouldn't lose a word of what they were saying."

"What were they saying?"

"That the moment they started to look for a lunatic they wouldn't have to go far to find him."

"I suppose they'd heard the scenes that took place up in your room."

"So what?"

She suddenly became almost furious and got up from her chair:

"Are you too, because he's fallen in love with a girl like

me and because he's jealous of me, are you going to presume that he's mad?"

Maigret got up in turn, tried, in order to calm her, to put his hand on her shoulder, but she pushed him away in anger.

"Say so, if that's how you see it."

"It is *not* how I see it."

"You think he's mad."

"Certainly not because he loves you."

"But he's mad all the same?"

"Until there's proof to the contrary, I've no reason for coming to that conclusion."

"What does that mean exactly?"

"It means that you're a good girl, and that . . . ."

"I'm not a good girl. I'm a whore, a piece of dirt, and I don't deserve . . . ."

"You're a good girl, and I promise you I'll do my best to discover the true culprit."

"Are you convinced it's not him?"

He sighed, embarrassed, and in order to hide his feelings began to light his pipe.

"So, you see, you don't dare say so!"

"You're a good girl, Louise. I shall probably come back again to see you. . . ."

But she had lost confidence and, on shutting the door behind him, she growled:

"You and your promises! . . ."

On the stairs, at the bottom of which the children were watching for him, he thought he heard her add to herself:

"You're nothing but a dirty policeman after all!"

5

At a quarter past eight, when they left the house on Rue Clemenceau, they almost shrank back in surprise at the suddenness with which so much calm and silence enveloped them.

Toward five in the afternoon, the sky had turned as black as at the Crucifixion, and lights had to be put on all over town. Two brief, rending claps of thunder had rung out, and at last the clouds had emptied themselves, not in rain, but in hail; people on the streets had disappeared, as though swept away by the squall, while white bullets rebounded on the cobblestones like Ping-Pong balls.

Maigret, who was in the Café de la Poste at that moment, had got to his feet with the rest, and everyone had remained standing by the windows, looking at the street as though they were watching a fireworks display.

Now, it was all over and it was a bit disconcerting to hear neither the rain nor the wind, to walk out in the still air, to see stars between the rooftops when one lifted one's head.

Possibly because of the silence, broken only by the sound of their footsteps, they walked without saying a word, going up the street toward Place Viète. Just at the corner of it, they almost bumped into a man standing motionless in the darkness, a white arm band on his overcoat, a club in his hand, who watched them pass without breathing a word.

A few steps farther on, Maigret was on the point of asking a question, and his friend, guessing this, explained in a constrained voice:

"The Police Superintendent telephoned me just before I left my office. It's been boiling up to this since yesterday. This morning, boys distributed notices in people's mailboxes. They held a meeting at six o'clock and have organized a watch committee."

"*They*" obviously did not refer to the boys but to the hostile elements in the town.

Chabot added:

"We can't prevent them from doing so."

Right outside the Vernoux' house, on Rue Rabelais, three more men with arm bands were standing on the sidewalk and watching them approach. They were not patrolling, simply standing there on guard, and one might almost have thought they were waiting for them, were perhaps going to keep them from entering. Maigret thought he recognized, in the smallest of the three, the thin figure of Chalus, the schoolmaster.

It was quite impressive. Chabot hesitated to go up to the entrance, was probably tempted to continue along the road. There was no sign as yet of a riot, or even a disturbance, but it was the first time they had come across such a tangible sign of public discontent.

Calm in appearance, very dignified, not without a kind of solemnity, the Examining Magistrate eventually mounted the steps and raised the door knocker.

Behind him, there wasn't a murmur, not even a joke. Still not moving, the three men watched what he did.

The noise of the knocker reverberated inside as though in a church. Immediately, as if he were there to await them, a butler manipulated the chains, the bolts, and received them in reverent silence.

It could not usually have been like this, because Julien Chabot paused on the threshold of the living room, sorry perhaps that he had come.

In a room the size of a ballroom, the great crystal chandelier was lit, other lights glittered on tables; enough armchairs were grouped in different corners, and around the fireplace, to seat forty people.

Yet only one man was there, at the farthest end of the room—Hubert Vernoux, with his silky white hair, who sprang from an immense Louis XIII armchair and came to meet them, hand outstretched.

"I told you yesterday, in the train, that you would be coming to see me, Monsieur Maigret. Besides, I telephoned today to our friend Chabot to make sure he would bring you."

He was dressed in black, and his coat was something like a dinner jacket; a monocle was dangling from a ribbon across his chest.

"My family will be here in a moment. I don't understand why they haven't all come down."

In the poor light of the train compartment, Maigret

had hardly seen him. Here, the man appeared older. When he had come across the room, his step had the mechanical stiffness of people with arthritis, whose movements seem controlled by springs. His face was puffy, almost artificially pink.

Why was the Chief Inspector reminded of an aged actor, forcing himself to go on playing his role and living in terror that the public will notice he's already half dead?

"I must have them told you're here."

He had rung, was addressing the butler.

"See if Madame is ready. Tell Mademoiselle Lucile too and the doctor and Madame . . ."

Something wasn't quite right. He was vexed with his family for not being there. To put him at ease, Chabot said, looking at the three bridge tables prepared:

"Is Henri de Vergennes going to come?"

"He excused himself by telephone. The storm has wrecked the drive of the château and he finds it impossible to get his car out."

"Aumale?"

"Our friend the lawyer developed flu this morning. He went to bed at midday."

Nobody would be coming, in fact. And it was as if the family itself were hesitating to come down. The butler hadn't reappeared. Hubert Vernoux pointed to the liqueurs on the table.

"Help yourselves, will you? I must ask you to excuse me for a moment."

He went to fetch them himself, climbed the great stone staircase, with its wrought-iron banisters.

"How many people usually come to these bridge parties?" Maigret inquired in a low voice.

"Not many. Five or six apart from the family."

"Who are usually in the living room when you arrive?"

Chabot nodded, reluctantly. Someone entered noiselessly, Dr. Alain Vernoux, who had not changed and was wearing the same creased suit he had had on in the morning.

"Are you alone?"

"Your father has just gone up."

"I met him on the staircase. What about the women?"

"I believe he's gone to call them."

"I don't think anyone else will come."

Alain jerked his head toward the windows, concealed by heavy curtains.

"You saw?"

And, knowing that they had understood what he meant:

"They're keeping watch on the house. There are probably some of them on guard by the door in the lane too. It's a very good thing."

"Why?"

"Because if another crime is committed, they won't be able to attribute it to someone in this house."

"Do you foresee another crime?"

"If it's a lunatic, there's no reason why the number should stop where it is."

Madame Vernoux, the doctor's mother, at last made her entrance, followed by her husband, who had a flushed face, as if he had had to argue to persuade her to come down. She was a woman of sixty, her hair still brown, with very dark-ringed eyes.

"Chief Inspector Maigret, of Police Headquarters in Paris."

She barely inclined her head, and went to sit down in an armchair, which must have been her own particular one. As she passed them, she merely greeted the Magistrate with a furtive:

"Good evening, Julien."

Hubert Vernoux announced:

"My sister-in-law will be down immediately. We had an electricity cut earlier, which made dinner late. I suppose the current was off all over town?"

He was talking for the sake of talking. It didn't matter what he said. He had to fill the void in the room.

"A cigar, Chief Inspector?"

For the second time since he had been in Fontenay, Maigret accepted one, because he didn't dare bring his pipe out of his pocket.

"Isn't your wife coming down?"

"She's probably being held up by the children."

It was obvious that Isabelle Vernoux, the mother, had consented to put in an appearance, after God knows what haggling, but that she was determined not to participate actively in the gathering. She had taken up her needlepoint and was not listening to what was being said.

"Do you play bridge, Chief Inspector?"

"I'm sorry to disappoint you, but I never play. I hasten to add that I get a great deal of pleasure just watching a game."

Hubert Vernoux looked at the Magistrate.

"How shall we play? Lucile will certainly play. You and I. I suppose, Alain . . ."

"No. Don't count on me."

"That leaves your wife. Would you go and see if she's nearly ready?"

It was becoming painful. Nobody, besides the mistress of the house, had decided to come down. Maigret's cigar enabled him to keep up appearances. Hubert Vernoux had also lit one up and was busy filling brandy glasses.

Could the three men standing guard outside guess that such things were happening indoors?

Lucile came down at last, and, though thinner and more angular, she was the image of her sister. She too accorded no more than a brief look at the Chief Inspector, walked straight to one of the card tables.

"Shall we begin?" she inquired.

Then, pointing vaguely at Maigret:

"Is he playing?"

"No."

"Who is playing, then? Why have you made me come down?"

"Alain has gone to fetch his wife."

"She won't come."

"Why not?"

"Because she's got one of her headaches. The children have been impossible the whole evening. The governess has given notice and left. Jeanne is looking after the baby. . . ."

Hubert Vernoux mopped his brow.

"Alain will persuade her."

And, turning to Maigret:

"I don't know if you have any children. No doubt it's the same in all big families. Everyone wants his own way. Everyone has his own pursuits, his particular likes . . ."

He was right: Alain brought in his wife, somewhat ordinary, rather dumpy, her eyes red from crying.

"Forgive me . . ." she said to her father-in-law. "The children have given me a lot of trouble."

"I gather that the governess . . ."

"We'll talk about it tomorrow."

"Chief Inspector Maigret . . ."

"I am delighted to meet you."

She offered her hand, but it was a limp hand, without warmth.

"Are we playing?"

"We are."

"Who?"

"You're sure, Chief Inspector, you don't want to take a hand?"

"Positive."

Julien Chabot, already seated, as if at home in the house, was shuffling the cards, stacking them up in the center of the green baize.

"It's your draw, Lucile."

She turned up a king, her brother-in-law a jack. The Magistrate and Alain's wife drew a three and a seven.

"We're partners."

All this had taken almost half an hour, but at last they were settled. In her corner, Isabelle Vernoux, the mother, looked at no one. Maigret was sitting in the background, behind Hubert Vernoux, whose hand he could see as well as that of his daughter-in-law.

"Pass."

"One club."

"Pass."

"One heart."

The doctor had remained standing, with the air of not knowing what to do. Everybody was as at his post. Hubert Vernoux had gathered them together, almost forcibly, to preserve an appearance of normal life in the house, perhaps for the Chief Inspector's benefit.

"Well now, Hubert?"

His sister-in-law, who was his partner, was calling him to order.

"Sorry! . . . Two clubs . . ."

"You're sure you shouldn't say three? I bid a heart against your club, which means I've at least two and a half honors. . . ."

From that moment Maigret began to be fascinated by the game. Not in the play itself, but in what it revealed to him of the players' characters.

His friend Chabot, for instance, was as steady as a metronome, his calls exactly what they should be, neither rash nor timid. He played his hand calmly, didn't pass a single remark to his partner. Barely a shade of annoyance came over his face when the young woman didn't respond correctly.

"I beg your pardon. I should have replied three spades."

"It doesn't matter. You couldn't know what I've got in my hand."

At the beginning of the third game, he bid, and succeeded in winning, a small slam, apologized for it:

"Too easy. I had it all in my hand."

The young woman herself was absent-minded, tried to pull herself together, and, when it was her turn to play, looked around her as though asking for help. Once she turned to Maigret, her fingers on a card, asking his advice.

She didn't like bridge, was only there because she had to be, to make up a fourth.

Lucile, on the other hand, dominated the table with her personality. It was she who, after each game, commented on the play and delivered sarcastic remarks.

"Since Jeanne bid two hearts, you should have known which way to finesse. She was bound to have the queen of hearts."

She was right, moreover. She was always right. Her little black eyes seemed to see through the cards.

"What's wrong with you today, Hubert?"

"Why? . . ."

"You're playing like a novice. You're hardly listening to the bids. We'd have been able to win that game with three no-trump and you ask for four clubs, which you can't manage."

"I expected you to say that. . . ."

"I didn't have to tell you about my diamonds. You should have . . ."

Hubert Vernoux tried to make up for it. He was like one of those roulette players who, once having lost, cling to the hope that their luck is going to turn any moment and try every number, furious to see the number come up that they have just abandoned.

Almost always, he bid beyond his own hand, relying on his partner's cards, and when they weren't there, he would bite the end of his cigar nervously.

"I assure you, Lucile, that I was perfectly entitled to call two spades right off."

"Except that you had neither the ace of spades nor the ace of diamonds."

"But I did have . . ."

He enumerated his cards, the blood rose to his head, while she regarded him with savage coldness.

To restore his losses, he bid still more recklessly, to the point where it was no longer bridge but poker.

Alain had gone to keep his mother company for a while. He came back to install himself behind the players, looking at the cards without interest, with his large eyes blurred by his glasses.

"Do you understand it at all, Chief Inspector?"

93

"I know the rules. I'm able to follow the game, but not play it."

"Does it interest you?"

"Greatly."

He scrutinized the Chief Inspector with more attention, seemed to realize that Maigret's interest lay much more in the behavior of the players than in the cards, and he watched his aunt and his father with a bored expression.

Chabot and Alain's wife won the first rubber.

"Shall we change?" Lucile suggested.

"Unless we take our revenge as we are."

"I'd sooner change partners."

This was a mistake on her part. She found herself playing with Chabot, who made no slips and with whom it was impossible for her to find fault. Jeanne was playing badly. But, perhaps because she invariably bid too low, Hubert Vernoux won two games in succession.

"It's luck, nothing else."

This was not quite true. He had had the cards, certainly. But if he hadn't bid with so much boldness, he would not have won, for he had no good reason to hope for the cards his partner held.

"Shall we continue?"

"Let's finish the round."

This time Vernoux was with the Magistrate, the two women together. And it was the men who won, which meant that Hubert Vernoux had won two rubbers out of three.

It seemed as if he was relieved, as though this bridge party had had considerable importance for him. He mopped his brow, went to pour himself a drink, brought a glass for Maigret.

"You see, in spite of what my sister-in-law says, I'm not so imprudent. What she doesn't understand is that if one manages to grasp the way in which one's opponent's mind works, one is halfway to winning the game, whatever the cards are. It's the same thing in selling a farm or a piece of land. Know what the buyer has in mind and . . ."

"Please, Hubert."

"What?"

"Couldn't you refrain from talking business here?"

"I'm sorry. I forgot that women like one to make money but prefer not to know how it's done."

This too was imprudent. His wife, from her distant armchair, called him to order.

"Have you been drinking?"

Maigret had seen him drink three or four cognacs. He had been struck by the way Vernoux filled his glass, furtively, as if in a hurry, in the hope that his wife and sister-in-law wouldn't see him. He would swallow the alcohol in one gulp, then, to reassure himself, would fill the Chief Inspector's glass.

"I've only had two glasses."

"They've gone to your head."

"I think," Chabot began, rising and taking his watch from his pocket, "it is time we left."

"It's hardly half past ten."

"You forget that I've a lot of work to do. My friend Maigret must be beginning to get tired too."

Alain seemed disappointed. Maigret felt sure that, all through the evening, the doctor had hung around him in the hope of drawing him into a corner.

The others didn't attempt to keep them. Hubert Vernoux didn't dare to insist. What would happen when the players departed and he was left alone with the three women? Because Alain did not count. That was obvious. Nobody bothered about him. Doubtless he would go up to his room or his laboratory. His wife was more a member of the family than he was.

It was a family of women, in fact; Maigret could see that right away. They had allowed Hubert Vernoux to play bridge on condition that he behave himself well, and they had continually watched him like a child.

Was this the reason why, outside his own home, he clung so desperately to the personality he had created for himself, attentive to the smallest sartorial details?

Who knows? Perhaps, earlier, when he had gone upstairs to fetch them, he had begged them to be nice to him, to allow him to play his role of master in the house without humiliating him with their remarks.

He was looking sidelong at the brandy decanter.

"One last glass, Chief Inspector? What the English call a *nightcap*?"

Maigret, who did not really want one, said yes in order to give him the opportunity to drink one as well, but while Vernoux was raising the glass to his lips, Maigret caught sight of his wife's fixed gaze, saw his hand hesitate, then, regretfully, put the glass down.

As the Magistrate and the Chief Inspector were reaching the door, where the butler was waiting for them with their coats, Alain murmured:

"Perhaps I'll accompany you part of the way."

He himself did not seem to be troubled by the women's reactions, though they seemed surprised. His own wife didn't object. It can't have made any difference to her whether he went out or not, seeing how little he counted in her life. She had gone over to her mother-in-law, whose work she was admiring, nodding her head up and down.

"You don't mind, Chief Inspector?"

"Not at all."

The night air was fresh, with a different freshness from that of the preceding nights, and one wanted to fill one's lungs, to greet the stars back in their places after so long.

The three men with arm bands were still on the sidewalk and, this time, they stepped back a pace to let them pass. Alain had not put on his overcoat. As he passed the coat stand, he had put on a soft felt hat, rendered shapeless by the recent storms.

Seen like this, his body leaning forward, his hands in his pockets, he was more like a student in his last year than a married man and father of a family.

On Rue Rabelais, they weren't able to talk, because voices carried a long way and they were conscious of the presence of the three watchers behind them. Alain jumped when he brushed against the one on guard at the corner of Place Viète, whom he hadn't seen.

"I suppose they've got them all over town?" he muttered.

"Definitely. They're going to work in shifts."

Few windows were still lighted. People were going to bed early. One could see, far down the long vista of Rue de la République, the lights in the Café de la Poste, still open, and two or three isolated people on the streets disappearing one after the other.

When they reached the Magistrate's house, they had still not had time to exchange a dozen sentences. Chabot murmured reluctantly:

"Will you come in?"

Maigret said no:

"No point in waking your mother."

"She won't be asleep. She never goes to bed before I'm back."

"We'll see each other tomorrow morning."

"Here?"

"I'll call at the Palais."

"I've a certain number of telephone calls to make before I go to bed. Maybe there'll be something new?"

"Good night, Chabot."

"Good night, Maigret. Good night, Alain."

They shook hands. The key turned in the lock; a moment later the door was shut again.

"May I come with you to the hotel?"

They were the only people in the street. For a split second, Maigret had a vision of the doctor taking his hand out of his pocket and knocking him on the skull with a hard object, a bit of lead piping or a wrench.

He replied:

"I'd be glad."

They set off. Alain could not bring himself to speak right away. When he did so, it was to ask:

"What do you think of it?"

"Of what?"

"Of Father."

What could Maigret reply? What was interesting was the fact that the question was being asked, that the young doctor had left his own home with no other reason than to ask it.

"I don't think he has had a happy life," the Chief Inspector murmured nonetheless, without much conviction.

"Are there people who do have a happy life?"

"For a while, at least. You are unhappy then, Monsieur Vernoux?"

"Oh, I don't count."

"Yet you try to get your share of pleasure."

The big eyes stared at him.

"What do you mean?"

"Nothing. Or, if you like, that totally unhappy people don't exist. Everyone clings to something, creates a kind of happiness for himself."

"Do you realize what that means?"

And, since Maigret did not reply:

"Do you know that it's this search for what I would call compensation, this search for some kind of happiness in spite of everything, that produces neurotics and, often, completely unbalanced people? The men who, at this moment, are drinking and playing cards at the Café de la Poste are trying to convince themselves that they are enjoying themselves there."

"And you?"

"I don't understand the question."

"Don't you look for compensation?"

This time, Alain was worried, suspected Maigret of knowing more, was reluctant to question him.

"Are you going to dare to go to the barracks district tonight?"

It was rather out of pity that the Chief Inspector asked that, in order to relieve him of his doubts.

"You know?"

"Yes."

"Have you talked to her?"

"For quite a time."

"What did she tell you?"

"Everything."

"Have I done wrong?"

"I'm not judging you. You're the one who brought up the subject of the instinctive quest for compensation. What are your father's compensations?"

They had lowered their voices, for they had reached the open door of the hotel, where a single light was on in the lobby.

"Why don't you answer?"

"Because I don't know the answer."

"Does he have no affairs?"

"Certainly not in Fontenay. He's too well known and it would get around."

"And you? Does it get around too?"

"No. My case isn't the same. When my father goes to Paris or Bordeaux, I suppose he treats himself to a little amusement."

He murmured to himself:

"Poor Papa!"

Maigret looked at him in surprise.

"Are you fond of your father?"

Modestly Alain replied:

"Anyhow, I'm sorry for him."

"Has it always been like that?"

"It's been worse. My mother and aunt have calmed down a bit."

"What have they got against him?"

"That he's a self-made man, the son of a cattle dealer who used to get drunk in village inns. The Courçons have never forgiven him for having needed him. Do you understand? And in the days of old Courçon his position was more painful, because Courçon was even more scathing than his daughters and his son, Robert. Until the death of my father, every Courçon in the land will re-proach him for the fact that they live off his money."

"How do they treat you, yourself?"

"As a Vernoux. And my wife, whose father was Vicomte de Cadeuil, is hand in glove with my mother and aunt."

"Did you intend to tell me all this, this evening?"

"I don't know."

"You meant to talk to me about your father?"

"I wanted to know what you thought of him."

"Weren't you chiefly anxious to know if I'd discovered the existence of Louise Sabati?"

"How did you find out?"

"Through an anonymous letter."

"Does the Magistrate know about it? The police?"

"They aren't doing anything about it."

"But will they?"

"Not if the murderer is discovered fairly soon. I have the letter in my pocket. I haven't spoken to Chabot about my interview with Louise."

"Why not?"

"Because I don't think, in the present state of the case, it has any bearing on it."

"She has nothing to do with it."

"Tell me, Monsieur Vernoux . . ."

"Yes."

"How old are you?"

"Thirty-six."

"How old were you when you finished your studies?"

"I left medical school at twenty-five and then I was a resident at Sainte-Anne for two years."

"You've never been tempted to live on your own?"

He seemed suddenly disheartened.

"Don't you want to answer?"

"I've nothing to answer. You wouldn't understand."

"Lack of courage?"

"I knew you would call it that."

"Nevertheless, you didn't return to Fontenay-le-Comte in order to look after your father?"

"Look, it's both simpler and more complicated than that. I came back one day to spend several weeks' vacation here."

"And you stayed on?"

"Yes."

"Aimlessly?"

"If you like. Though it's not exactly that."

"You felt you couldn't do anything else?"

Alain dropped the subject.

"How is Louise?"

"The same as ever, I imagine."

"She isn't worried?"

"Is it long since you saw her?"

"Two days. I went to her house yesterday evening. After that, I didn't dare. Nor today. This evening, it's worse, with men patrolling the streets. Do you understand why it is, since the first murder, public opinion has turned against us?"

"It's a phenomenon I've often noted."

"Why choose us?"

"Whom do you think they suspect? Your father or you?"

"It doesn't matter to them so long as it's one of the family. My mother or aunt would suit them just as well."

They had to stop talking because steps were approaching. It was two men with arm bands and clubs, who took stock of them as they passed. One of them shone the beam of a flashlight on them and, as they moved off, said in a loud voice to his companion:

"It's Maigret."

"The other is Vernoux's son."

"I recognized him."

The Chief Inspector advised his companion:

"You'd better go home."

"Yes."

"And don't get involved with them."

"Thank you."

"For what?"

"Oh, nothing."

He didn't hold out his hand. His hat on one side, he went off, bent forward, in the direction of the bridge, and the patrol, which had stopped, watched him pass in silence.

Maigret shrugged his shoulders, went into the hotel, and waited for someone to hand him his key. There were two letters for him, probably anonymous, but neither the paper nor the handwriting was the same.

6

When he realized it was Sunday, he began to dawdle. Even before this, he had been playing a secret game from his early childhood. He occasionally played it still, in bed beside his wife, taking care that she should guess nothing. And she would be taken in, saying, when she brought him his cup of coffee:

"What were you dreaming of?"

"Why?"

"You were smiling in your sleep."

This morning, at Fontenay, before opening his eyes, he felt a ray of sunshine passing through his eyelids. He didn't merely feel it. He had the impression of seeing it through the fine skin, which was tingling, and, probably because of the blood circulating there, it was a sun redder than the one in the sky, glorious, as in a painting.

He could create a whole world with this sun, showers of sparks, volcanoes, cascades of melted gold. He simply had to keep his eyelids moving lightly like a kaleidoscope, using his lashes as a grid.

He heard pigeons cooing on a cornice above his window, then bells ringing from two directions at once, and he could imagine the steeples pointing up into the sky, which was surely an unclouded blue today.

He went on with his game, all the while listening to the noises in the street, and it was then, from the echo that lingered after footsteps, from a certain quality of the silence, that he recognized it was Sunday.

He hesitated some time before stretching out his arm to reach his watch on the bedside table. It showed half past nine. In Paris, on Boulevard Richard-Lenoir, if spring had at last reached there too, Madame Maigret would certainly have opened the windows and tidied the room, in dressing gown and slippers, while a stew would be simmering on the stove.

He promised himself he would telephone her. Since there were no telephones in the bedrooms, he would have to wait until he went down, and call her from the telephone booth.

He pressed the electric bell. He thought the chambermaid looked neater, jollier than on the day before.

"What would you like to eat?"

"Nothing. I want a lot of coffee."

She had the same curious way of looking at him.

"Shall I run you a bath?"

"Not until I've finished my coffee."

He lit a pipe, went to open the window. The air was still sharp—he had to put on his dressing gown—but little waves of warmth could already be felt. The façades of houses and the roads had dried out. The street was deserted, except now and again for a family going by in their Sunday best, a country woman holding a bunch of mauve lilacs in her hand.

The life of the hotel must have slowed down, for he had to wait a long time for his coffee. He had left the two letters he had received the night before on the bedside table. One of them was signed. The handwriting was as neat as on an engraving, in black ink like India ink.

"Are you aware that the widow Gibon was the midwife who delivered Madame Vernoux of her son Alain?

"It may be useful to know.

"Best wishes.

"Anselme Remouchamps."

The second letter, anonymous, had been written on a sheet of paper of excellent quality, the top of which had been cut off, doubtless to remove the imprint. It was written in pencil.

"Why don't you question the servants? They know more about it than anyone."

When he had read these two lines, the previous evening, before going to bed, Maigret had had an intuition that they had been written by the butler at Rue Rabelais, who had received him without a word and who at his departure had handed him his overcoat. The man, dark-complexioned, strongly built, was between forty and fifty years of age. He gave the impression of being a farmer's son who has refused to cultivate the land, and who harbors as much hatred for rich people as he pours scorn on the peasants from whom he has sprung.

It would probably be easy to obtain a specimen of his handwriting. Perhaps the paper was even the Vernouxs' own?

106

All this had to be checked. In Paris, the task would have been simple. Here, actually, it was no business of his.

When the chambermaid came in at last with the coffee, he asked her:

"Are you from Fontenay?"

"I was born on Rue des Loges."

"Do you know anyone called Remouchamps?"

"The shoemaker?"

"His Christian name's Anselme."

"He's the shoemaker who lives two doors away from my mother; he has a wart on his nose as big as a pigeon's egg."

"What sort of man is he?"

"He's been a widower for I don't know how many years. I've always known him as a widower. He leers strangely when girls go by to frighten them."

She looked at him in surprise.

"Do you smoke your pipe before drinking your coffee?"

"You may get my bath ready."

He went to have it in the bathroom at the end of the hall and spent a long time in the warm water, daydreaming. Several times he opened his mouth as if to speak to his wife, whom, when he was having a bath, he usually heard going to and fro in the next room.

It was quarter past ten when he went downstairs. The hotel proprietor was behind the desk, in consultation with the cook.

"The Examining Magistrate telephoned twice."

"At what time?"

"The first time, a little after nine o'clock, the second a few minutes ago. The second time he called I replied that it wouldn't be very long before you were down."

"May I make a call to Paris?"

"Being Sunday, perhaps it won't take long."

He gave his number, went to take the air outside the front door. There was no one there, today, to watch him. A cock crowed somewhere, not far off, and one could hear the waters of the Vendée flowing past. When an old woman in a mauve hat came by, he would have sworn he caught a whiff of incense from her clothes.

It was well and truly Sunday.

"Hello! Is that you?"

"You're still at Fontenay? Are you telephoning from Chabot's? How is his mother?"

Instead of replying, he inquired in turn:

"What's the weather like in Paris?"

"Since midday yesterday it's been spring."

"Midday yesterday?"

"Yes. It began immediately after lunch."

He had lost half a day of sunshine!

"And what's it like there?"

"It's fine too."

"You haven't caught a cold?"

"I'm very well."

"Are you coming back tomorrow morning?"

"I think so."

"Aren't you sure? I thought . . ."

"I may be detained a few hours."

"What with?"

"Some work."

"You told me . . ."

. . . That he would seize the chance of having a rest, of course! Wasn't he having a rest?

That was practically all. They exchanged the remarks they usually exchanged by telephone.

After which he rang Chabot at his home. Rose answered that the Magistrate had left for the Palais at eight in the morning. He called the Palais de Justice.

"Anything new?"

"Yes. They have recovered the weapon. That's why I called you. They told me you were asleep. Can you come up here?"

"I'll be along in a few minutes."

"The gates are closed. I'll watch out for you at the window and let you in."

"Has something gone wrong?"

Chabot's voice on the phone seemed dejected.

"I'll talk to you about it."

Maigret nonetheless took his time. He was determined to savor the Sunday and was soon walking slowly along Rue de la République, where the Café de la Poste had already set out its chairs and little yellow tables on the terrace.

Two houses farther on, the baker's shop door was open, and Maigret slowed down still more to inhale the sugary smell.

The bells were ringing. There was starting to be more life on the street, roughly opposite Julien Chabot's house. It was the crowd beginning to come out of the half past ten mass at the church of Notre Dame. It seemed to him that the people were not behaving quite as they would on other Sundays. There weren't many of the faithful making straight for home.

Groups were forming in the square; they were not arguing noisily but talking in low voices, often stopping completely as they watched the doors out of which the stream of parishioners was flowing. Even the women were in no hurry, holding their gilt-edged missals in their gloved hands, and almost all of them were wearing bright spring hats.

Outside the porch stood a long, gleaming motorcar, with, standing by its door, a chauffeur in black uniform whom Maigret recognized as the Vernouxs' butler.

Did these people, who lived no more than four hundred yards away, generally drive to high mass by car? It was possible. It was, perhaps, part of their tradition. It was also possible that they had taken the car today in order to avoid contact with inquisitive people in the streets.

They were just coming out, and the white head of Hubert Vernoux stood out above the others. He was walking with slow steps, his hat in his hand. When he reached the top of the steps, Maigret recognized, beside him, his wife, sister-in-law, and daughter-in-law.

The crowd dispersed imperceptibly. Strictly speaking they didn't clear the way, but there was, nevertheless, a wide space around them, and all eyes converged on their group.

The chauffeur opened the door. The women entered first. Then Hubert took his place on the front seat and the limousine glided off in the direction of Place Viète.

Perhaps at that moment, a word uttered by someone in the crowd, a shout, a gesture would have sufficed to make popular fury assert itself. Anywhere else than at the exit from church it might well have happened. People's faces were hard, and though the clouds had been swept from the sky, there yet remained a sense of unrest in the air.

A few people greeted the Chief Inspector timidly. Did

they still trust him? They watched as he, in his turn, went up the street, his pipe in his mouth, his shoulders hunched.

He circled around Place Viète, turned onto Rue Rabelais. Outside the Vernoux' on the opposite sidewalk, two young men, not yet twenty, were standing guard. They didn't wear arm bands, carried no clubs. These accessories seemed reserved for the night patrols. Still, they were on duty and they showed themselves proud of it.

One of them raised his cap to Maigret as he went by, but not the other.

Six or seven newspapermen were grouped on the steps of the Palais de Justice, where the big gates were closed, and Lomel had sat down, his cameras placed beside him.

"Do you think they'll let you in?" he called to Maigret. "Have you heard the news?"

"What news?"

"It seems they've found the weapon. They're in full session in there."

The gate half opened, Chabot signed to Maigret to come in quickly, and, as soon as he had passed through, pushed back the gate as if he feared a mass invasion of reporters.

The hallways were gloomy and all the dampness of the past few weeks clung to the stone walls.

"I would like to have spoken to you, privately, first, but it was impossible."

It was brighter in the Magistrate's office. The Public Prosecutor was there, sitting in a chair which he was tipping backward, a cigarette in his mouth. Superintendent Féron was there too, as well as Inspector Chabiron, who could not help throwing Maigret a look at once triumphant and mocking.

111

On the desk, the Chief Inspector saw immediately a piece of lead piping, about nine inches long and two inches in diameter.

"Is that it?"

Everybody nodded in assent.

"No fingerprints?"

"Only some traces of blood and two or three hairs stuck to it."

The pipe, painted dark green, had once been part of the plumbing in a kitchen or a cellar or garage. It had been cleanly cut off, in all probability by a professional several months before, because the metal had had time to tarnish.

Had the length been cut when someone was removing a sink or some other such fitting? It was possible.

Maigret was on the point of asking where the object had been discovered when Chabot spoke:

"Tell your story, Inspector."

Chabiron, who was only waiting for the signal, put on a modest look:

"We, in Poitiers, still stick to the good old methods. With the result that I, and my colleague, have questioned everyone living on the street, I've searched in every nook and cranny. A few yards from the place where Gobillard was attacked, there's a big door leading into a yard belonging to a horse dealer and surrounded by stables. This morning, I was curious enough to go and look there. And, in the midst of the manure all over the ground, I soon found the object you see there. The chances are that the murderer, on hearing footsteps, threw it over the wall."

"Who examined it for fingerprints?"

"I did. Superintendent Féron helped me. We may not be experts, but we know enough to take fingerprints. It's certain that Gobillard's murderer was wearing gloves. As regards the hairs, we went to the morgue in order to compare them with those of the dead man."

He concluded with satisfaction:

"They match."

Maigret took care not to give any opinion. There was a pause, which the Magistrate finally broke.

"We were in the middle of discussing what it would be best to do now. This discovery appears, at least at first sight, to confirm Emile Chalus's statement."

Maigret still said nothing.

"If the weapon had not been discovered on those premises, one could have maintained that it would have been difficult for the doctor to have got rid of it before going to telephone at the Café de la Poste. As the Inspector points out, with good reason . . ."

Chabiron decided to say what he thought himself:

"Let us suppose that the murderer had, in fact, gone away, having committed his crime, before the arrival of Alain Vernoux, as the latter claims. It is his third crime. The other two times he took the weapon away with him. Not only have we found nothing on Rue Rabelais, or on Rue des Loges, but it seems evident that he dealt the blow on all three occasions with the same piece of lead piping."

Maigret had realized this already, but he deemed it better to let him continue.

"The man had no reason, this last time, to throw the weapon over a wall. He wasn't being followed. Nobody had seen him. But if we admit that the doctor is the murderer, it was essential that he get rid of such a compromising object before . . ."

"Why tell the authorities?"

"Because that would put him in the clear. He thought no one would suspect the man who gave the alarm."

This seemed logical too.

"That's not all. As you know very well."

He had pronounced these last words with a certain embarrassment, because Maigret, without being his immediate superior, was nevertheless a gentleman whom one does not attack directly.

"Go on, Féron."

The Police Superintendent, embarrassed, first of all stubbed out his cigarette in the ashtray. Chabot, gloomily, avoided looking at his friend. Only the Public Prosecutor, who looked every now and again at his wristwatch, seemed like a man with more agreeable things to do.

After a cough, the little Police Superintendent turned toward Maigret.

"When, yesterday, somebody telephoned me to inquire whether I knew a girl named Sabati . . ."

The Chief Inspector knew what had happened and was suddenly afraid. He had an unpleasant sensation in his chest and his pipe began to taste nasty.

". . . I wondered, naturally, if it had any connection with the case. It struck me again only toward the middle of the afternoon. I was busy. I was on the point of sending one of my men; then I thought I might call to see her, on the off chance, on my way to dinner."

"Did you go there?"

"I heard you had seen her before me."

Féron lowered his head, as though it upset him to bring an accusation.

"She told you so?"

"Not right away. At first she refused to open the door to me and I had to resort to drastic measures."

"Did you threaten her?"

"I told her she might have to pay dearly for playing such games. She let me in. I noticed her black eye. I asked her who had done it. For over half an hour she kept as tight as a clam, watching me suspiciously. It was then that I decided to take her to the police station, where it's easier to make *them* speak."

Maigret felt weighed down, not just because of what had happened to Louise Sabati, but because of the Superintendent's attitude. In spite of his hesitations, his apparent humility, the man was fundamentally very proud of what he had done.

One could tell he had blithely set upon this uneducated girl who had no means of defense. Yet he must have come from common stock himself. He had taken it out on one of his own kind.

Almost every word he uttered now, in a voice increasingly assured, was hateful to hear.

"The fact that she hasn't worked for more than eight months means she is legally without means of support; this was the first thing I pointed out to her. And because she receives a man regularly, that ranks her in the category of prostitutes. She understood. She was afraid. She fought back for a long time. I don't know how you fixed it, but she finally confessed that she had told you all."

"All what?"

"Her relationship with Alain Vernoux, his behavior, how he fell into blind rages of passion and beat her black and blue."

"Did she spend the night in a cell?"

"I released her this morning. It's done her some good."

"Did she sign her statement?"

"I wouldn't have let her go without that."

Chabot addressed a look of reproach to his friend.

"I knew nothing of this," he murmured.

He had probably said so to them already; Maigret had not told him of his visit to the neighborhood of the barracks. Now, the Magistrate probably considered this silence, which put him in an awkward position, a betrayal.

Maigret remained outwardly composed. His glance wandered musingly over the little weak-looking Superintendent, who seemed to be waiting for congratulations.

"I suppose you have drawn some conclusions from this story?"

"It puts Doctor Vernoux, at any rate, in a new light. This morning, early, I interrogated the women neighbors, who confirmed that, at almost every one of his visits, violent scenes broke out in her rooms, to such an extent that several times they almost called the police."

"Why didn't they do so?"

"Probably because they thought it was no concern of theirs."

No! If the women neighbors did not raise the alarm, it was because it gave them satisfaction that the Sabati girl, who had nothing to do all day, should be beaten. And, probably, the more Alain hit her, the more pleased they were.

They might have been sisters of little Superintendent Féron.

"What's become of her now?"

"I instructed her to return home and to consider herself under the Examining Magistrate's orders."

The latter coughed as well.

"Certainly this morning's two discoveries put Alain Vernoux in a difficult spot."

"What did he do last night when he left me?"

It was Féron who replied:

"He returned to his home. I'm in touch with the watch committee. Since I couldn't prevent this committee from forming, I have thought it best to assure myself of its collaboration. Vernoux returned home right away."

"Does he usually attend mass at half past ten?"

Chabot, this time, replied.

"He doesn't go to mass at all. He's the only one of the family not to do so."

"Did he go out this morning?"

Féron made a vague gesture.

"I don't think so. At half past nine nothing had as yet been reported to me."

The Public Prosecutor at last joined in the conversation, as though he were beginning to feel he had had enough of it.

"All this is getting us nowhere. What we need to know is whether we have enough charges against Alain Vernoux to put him under arrest."

He stared hard at the Magistrate.

"It concerns you, Chabot. It's your responsibility."

Chabot, in turn, looked at Maigret, whose expression remained solemn and neutral.

Then, instead of replying, the Examining Magistrate delivered a speech.

"The situation is as follows. For one reason or another, public opinion has pointed to Alain Vernoux, ever since the first murder, that of his uncle Robert de Courçon. I am still wondering on what grounds people have adopted this attitude. Alain Vernoux isn't popular. His family is more or less disliked. Indeed, I've received twenty anonymous letters referring to the house on Rue Rabelais and accusing me of being in league with the rich people with whom I have social contacts.

"The other two crimes have not lessened these suspicions; far from it. For a long time, Alain Vernoux has been considered by certain people as 'a man apart.' "

Féron interrupted him:

"The Sabati girl's statement . . ."

". . . is damning for him, as is Chalus's statement, now that the weapon has been retrieved. Three crimes in one week is a lot. It's natural that the townspeople are worried and seeking to protect themselves. Up to the present time, I have hesitated to act, judging the evidence insufficient. Indeed, as the Public Prosecutor has just remarked, it's a heavy responsibility. As soon as he is put under arrest, a man of Vernoux's character, even if guilty, will tell nothing."

He surprised a smile, which was not without irony or bitterness, on Maigret's lips, blushed, lost the thread of his ideas.

"The question is whether it's better to arrest him now or wait for . . ."

Maigret could not help muttering between his teeth:

"They arrested the Sabati girl and shut her up the whole night, all right!"

Chabot heard him, was about to answer, probably to retort that it wasn't the same thing, but at the last moment changed his mind.

"This morning, because it's a fine Sunday, because of mass, we are experiencing a sort of respite. But by this time, at their apéritifs, in the cafés, people will have started talking again. Some of them, going for a walk, will deliberately go past the Vernouxs' house. It's known that I played bridge there yesterday evening and that the Chief Inspector accompanied me. It's hard to make them understand . . ."

"Are you going to arrest him?" the Public Prosecutor inquired, rising to his feet, thinking the beating about the bush had lasted long enough.

"I'm afraid that, as tonight comes on, there may be an incident that could have grave consequences. It needs only the smallest thing, a youngster throwing a stone at the windows, a drunkard starting to shout insults outside the house. In the present state of public feeling . . ."

"Are you going to arrest him?"

The Public Prosecutor was looking for his hat, couldn't find it. The little Superintendent, obsequiously, was saying to him:

"You left it in your study. I'll go and get it for you."

And Chabot, turning to Maigret, was murmuring:

"What do you think?"

"Nothing."

"In my shoes, what . . . ?"

"I'm not in your shoes."

"Do you believe the doctor is mad?"

"That depends on what you call mad."

"That he's the murderer?"

Maigret did not reply, looked for his hat too.

"Wait a moment. I've something to talk to you about. First, I must finish this. It can't be helped if I'm wrong."

He opened the drawer on the right, took from it a printed form, which he began to fill in, while Chabiron threw a look at Maigret more mocking than ever.

Chabiron and the little Superintendent had won. The

form was a warrant for arrest. Chabot hesitated yet another second on the point of signing it and adding the official stamp.

Then he wondered to which of the two men to hand it. Such an arrest as this had never occurred before in Fontenay.

"I suppose . . ."

At last:

"Anyway, you can both go. As discreetly as possible, to avoid demonstrations. You'd better take a car."

"I've got my own," Chabiron put in.

It was an unpleasant moment. It seemed, for a few seconds, that everyone felt a little ashamed. Perhaps not so much because they doubted the doctor's guilt, of which they felt pretty sure, but because they knew, deep down in themselves, that it was not on account of his guilt that they were acting, but from fear of public opinion.

"Keep me informed," muttered the Public Prosecutor, who went out first and added:

"If I'm not at home, call me at my parents-in-laws' house."

He was going to spend the rest of Sunday with his family. In their turn, Féron and Chabiron left, and it was the little Superintendent who had the warrant carefully folded in his wallet.

Chabiron retraced his steps, after a glance out the hall window, to ask:

"What about the press?"

"Don't say anything to them now. Make for the center of town first. You can tell them that I'll have a statement to make from here in half an hour, and they'll stay here."

"Are we to bring him here?"

"Straight to the prison. In case the crowd should be

tempted to lynch him, it will be easier to protect him there."

All this took some time. They were at last alone. Chabot was not proud of himself.

"What do you think of it?" he decided to inquire. "D'you think I'm wrong?"

"I am afraid," admitted Maigret, who was smoking his pipe, looking gloomy.

"Of what?"

He did not reply.

"In all conscience, I couldn't act otherwise."

"I know. It's not that I am thinking about."

"About what then?"

He did not want to admit that it was the attitude of the little Superintendent toward Louise Sabati that lay heavy on his heart.

Chabot looked at his watch.

"In half an hour, it will be over. We'll be able to go and question him."

Maigret continued to say nothing, as though he were following God knows what mysterious thoughts.

"Why didn't you tell me about it, yesterday evening?"

"About the Sabati girl?"

"Yes."

"To try to avoid what's happened."

"It's happened all the same."

"Yes. I didn't foresee that Féron would do anything about it."

"Have you got the letter?"

"Which letter?"

"The anonymous letter I received about her and that I handed to you. Now, I'm obliged to put it in the file."

Maigret searched his pockets, found it, crumpled, still

damp from last night's rain, and dropped it on the desk.

"Would you mind seeing if the journalists have followed them?"

He went to glance out the window. The reporters and photographers were still there, looking as if they expected something to happen.

"Have you the right time?"

"Five past twelve."

They had not heard the chimes sound. With all the doors shut, they were as though in a cellar there, where not a ray of sun could penetrate.

"I wonder how he will react. I wonder too what his father . . ."

The telephone rang suddenly. Chabot was so taken aback that for a moment he sat still, without answering it, at last muttered, staring at Maigret:

"Hello . . ."

He frowned, his eyebrows puckered:

"Are you sure?"

Maigret could hear the noise of a loud voice coming from the receiver, without being able to make out the words. It was Chabiron speaking.

"Have you searched the house? . . . Where are you at the moment? . . . Good. . . . Yes. Stay there. I . . ."

He passed his hand over his head in anguish.

"I'll call you back in a few minutes."

When he hung up, Maigret contented himself with one word.

"Gone?"

"Were you expecting it?"

And, when he didn't reply:

"He returned home last night immediately after leaving you; that we know for certain. He spent the night in his room. This morning, early, he asked for a cup of coffee to be brought up to him."

"And the newspapers."

"We have no papers on Sunday."

"To whom did he speak?"

"I don't know yet. Féron and the Inspector are still in the house and questioning the servants. Shortly after ten o'clock the whole family, except Alain, set off for mass in the car, driven by the butler."

"I saw them."

"On their return, no one worried about the doctor. It's a house where, except on Saturday evening, everyone lives in his own quarters. When my two men arrived, a maid went up to inform Alain. He wasn't in his room. They called all over the house for him. Do you think he has run away?"

"What does the man on guard in the street say?"

"Féron questioned him. It seems that the doctor left shortly after the rest of the family and went down into town on foot."

"Wasn't he followed? I thought . . ."

"I had given instructions he should be followed. Perhaps the police thought that on Sunday morning it wasn't necessary. I don't know. If they don't catch him, they'll make out that I allowed him time to escape on purpose."

"They'll certainly say so."

"There's no train before five o'clock this afternoon. Alain hasn't a car."

"So he can't be very far."

"You think so?"

"It wouldn't surprise me if they found him at his mis-

123

tress's. Normally, he slips out to see her only in the evenings, under cover of darkness. But it's three days since he saw her."

Maigret did not add that Alain knew he had been to see her.

"What's wrong?" the Examining Magistrate inquired.

"Nothing. I am afraid, that's all. You'd better send them over there."

Chabot telephoned. After which, both of them sat in silence, face to face, in the office where spring had not yet entered and where the green lampshade gave them a sickly look.

7

While they were waiting, Maigret suddenly had the embarrassing impression that he was watching his friend through a magnifying glass. Chabot appeared to him even older, more worn out than when he had arrived the night before last. There was just enough life, energy, personality in him, to lead the kind of existence he had been leading, and when, unexpectedly, as was the case now, he was called upon to make an extra effort, he collapsed, ashamed of his listlessness.

Yet, the Chief Inspector was sure it was not just a question of age. He must always have been like that. It was Maigret who had been mistaken, long ago, during the time they had been students and he had been envious of his friend. Chabot had then been for him the symbol of happy adolescence. At Fontenay, a mother, full of little attentions to him, was there to welcome him in a comfortable house, where everything had a robust, permanent appearance. He knew he would inherit, aside from that house, two or three farms and he received enough money each month to be able to lend some to his friends.

Thirty years had passed and Chabot had become what he was bound to become. Today, it was he who was turning to Maigret for help.

The minutes passed. The Magistrate made a pretense of glancing through a file but his eyes were not following the typewritten lines. The telephone still didn't ring.

He drew his watch from his pocket.

"It takes only five minutes to get there by car. The same again to return. They should have . . ."

It was a quarter past twelve. One had to allow the two men a few minutes for looking through the house.

"If he doesn't confess, and if, in two or three days, I haven't discovered undeniable proof against him, I'll be simply obliged to ask for my retirement to be moved forward."

He had acted through fear of the bulk of the population. At the moment, it was the reactions of the Vernouxs and their social equals that frightened him.

"Twenty past twelve. I wonder what they're doing."

At twenty-five past twelve he got up, too nervous to remain sitting.

"Haven't you got a car?" the Chief Inspector asked him.

He seemed embarrassed.

"I had one, which I used on Sundays to take my mother for drives in the country."

It was odd to hear someone speak of the country when

126

living in a town where cows were grazing only five hundred yards from the main street.

"Now that my mother no longer goes out except for mass on Sunday, what would I go with a car?"

Had he, perhaps, grown mean? It was quite likely. Not so much through his own fault. When one owns a tidy little property like his, one is inevitably scared of losing it.

Maigret felt that, since his arrival in Fontenay, he had come to understand things about which he had never thought, and he was building up a different picture of a small town from that which he had imagined until then.

"Something's certainly happened."

The two policemen had left more than twenty minutes ago. It wouldn't take long to search Louise Sabati's two-room lodging. Vernoux was not the kind of man to make his escape by a window, and it was hard to imagine a manhunt taking place in the streets around the barracks.

There was a moment of hope when they heard the engine of a car climbing the sloping street, and the Magistrate stood still, expectant, but the car passed without stopping.

"I give up."

He pulled his long fingers, covered with pale hairs, threw brief glances at Maigret as though begging him to reassure him, while the Chief Inspector persisted in remaining inscrutable.

When, a little after half past twelve, the telephone rang at last, Chabot literally threw himself at the instrument.

"Hello!" he cried.

But, immediately, he was discomfited. A woman's voice could be heard, a woman who was probably unused to the telephone and spoke so loud that the Chief

Inspector could hear her from the other side of the room.

"Is that the Magistrate?"

"Yes, the Examining Magistrate, Chabot. Speaking."

She repeated in the same tone of voice:

"Is it the Magistrate?"

"Yes, of course! What is it you want?"

"You are the Magistrate?"

And he, furious:

"Yes. I am the Magistrate. Can't you hear me?"

"No."

"What do you want?"

If she had asked him once more if he was the Magistrate, he would probably have thrown the instrument on the floor.

"The Superintendent wants you to come."

"What do you mean?"

But now, speaking to someone else, in the room from where she was telephoning, she said in a different voice:

"I've told him. What?"

Someone ordered:

"Hang up."

"Hang up what?"

A noise was heard in the Palais de Justice. Chabot and Maigret pricked up their ears.

"Someone's knocking loudly at the door."

"Come on."

They ran down the hallways. The knocking redoubled. Chabot hurriedly pulled the bolt and turned the key in the lock.

"Did they call you?"

It was Lomel, in the midst of three or four of his colleagues. They could see others going up the street in the direction of the open country.

"Chabiron has just gone past, driving his car. There was an unconscious woman beside him. He must have been taking her to the hospital."

A car was parked at the foot of the steps.

"Whose is that?"

"Mine, or, rather, my newspaper's," said a Bordeaux reporter.

"Will you drive us?"

"To the hospital?"

"No. First of all, go down to Rue de la République. Turn right, toward the barracks."

They all piled into the car. Outside the Vernouxs' house, a score of people had gathered, who watched them pass in silence.

"What's happening, Magistrate?" Lomel asked.

"I don't know. An arrest should have been made."

"The doctor?"

He hadn't the courage to say no, to carry on a battle of wits. A few people were sitting on the terrace of the Café de la Poste. A woman, in her Sunday clothes, was coming out of the pastry shop with a white cardboard box suspended from her finger by a piece of red string.

"That way?"

"Yes. Now, to the left ... Wait ... Turn just past that building. ..."

There was no mistaking it. Outside the house in which Louise had her rooms a swarm of people, mostly women and children, who rushed to the doors when the car stopped. The fat woman who had answered Maigret the evening before stood in the front row, her hands on her hips.

"It was me who went to phone you from the grocer's. The Superintendent's upstairs."

129

It was developing into confusion. The little company of people went around to the back of the house; Maigret, who knew the way, took the lead.

The onlookers, more numerous on this side, were blocking the outside door. There were even some of them on the stairs, at the top of which the little Police Superintendent had been obliged to mount guard in front of the broken-down door.

"Make room . . . Stand aside . . ."

Féron's face had fallen, his hair over his forehead. He had lost his hat somewhere. He seemed relieved that he had been rescued.

"Have you told the police station to send me help?"

"I didn't know that . . ." the Magistrate began to say.

"I instructed that woman to tell you . . ."

The newspapermen were trying to take photographs. A baby was crying. Chabot, whom Maigret had made go ahead, reached the last few steps as he asked:

"What's going on?"

"He's dead."

He pushed the wooden door, which had been partly shattered.

"In the bedroom."

The room was in disorder. Sunshine and flies were entering through the open window.

On the unmade bed, Dr. Alain Vernoux was lying, fully dressed, his glasses on the pillow next to his face, which already looked bloodless.

"Tell us, Féron."

"There's nothing to tell. We arrived, the Inspector and I, and were shown to this staircase. We knocked. When no one answered, I issued the usual orders. Chabiron

130

used his shoulder two or three times on the door. We found him just as he is, where he is. I tested his pulse. It was no longer beating. I placed a mirror in front of his mouth."

"And the girl?"

"She was on the floor, as though she had slipped off the bed, and she had been sick."

They were all treading on what she had thrown up.

"She wasn't moving, but she wasn't dead. There's no telephone in the house. I couldn't run around the neighborhood searching for one. Chabiron carried her over his shoulder and took her off to the hospital. There was nothing else to do."

"You are sure she was breathing?"

"Yes, with a strange rattle in her throat."

The photographers were still busy. Lomel was taking notes in a little red book.

"The whole building descended on me. At one time, some kids managed to slink their way into the room. I couldn't leave here. I wanted to warn you. I sent the woman who appears to act as concierge, instructing her to tell you . . ."

Indicating the disorder around him, he added:

"I haven't even glanced over the rooms."

It was one of the reporters who held up an empty tube of Veronal.

"Anyway, there's this."

It was the explanation. As far as Alain Vernoux was concerned, it was surely a case of suicide.

Had he persuaded Louise to kill herself with him? Had he administered the drug to her without saying anything?

In the kitchen, a mug of coffee still contained some

liquid at the bottom, and they saw a bit of cheese beside a slice of bread, with a piece bitten out of the bread by the girl.

She used to get up late. Alain Vernoux must have found her in the middle of eating her breakfast.

"Was she dressed?"

"In her nightdress. Chabiron rolled her up in a blanket and carried her off like that."

"The neighbors didn't hear a quarrel?"

"I haven't been able to question them. The kids are always hanging around in front and the mothers do nothing to shift them away. Listen to them."

One of the reporters had his back against the door, which could no longer be shut, to prevent it from being pushed from outside.

Julien Chabot was going to and fro as if in a bad dream, like a man who has lost control of the situation.

Two or three times, he went over to the corpse before daring to put his hand on the dangling wrist.

He repeated several times, forgetting he had already said it, or determined to convince himself:

"It's obviously suicide."

Then he asked:

"Shouldn't Chabiron be coming back?"

"I presume he'll stay there to question the girl if she recovers consciousness. He would have had to notify the police station. Chabiron promised to send me a doctor. . . ."

Here he was, knocking on the door, a young intern, who went right over to the bed.

"Dead?"

He nodded his head.

"What about the girl who was brought to you?"

"They're seeing to her. She's got a chance of pulling through."

He looked at the tube, shrugged his shoulders, muttered:

"Always the same stuff."

"How is it he's dead, if she . . ."

He pointed to the vomit on the floor.

One of the reporters, who had disappeared without anyone noticing, came back into the room.

"There wasn't a quarrel," he said. "I've questioned the neighbors. They can be all the more sure about it because most rooms had their windows open this morning."

Lomel himself was unabashedly rummaging through the drawers, which didn't contain much, underclothes and cheap dresses, knickknacks of no value. Then he bent down to look under the bed, and Maigret saw him lie flat on the floor, stretch out his arm, bring out a cardboard shoe box, with a blue ribbon around it. Lomel withdrew to one side with his find, and there was enough confusion for him to be left alone in peace.

It was only Maigret who went up to him.

"What is it?"

"Some letters."

The box was practically full of them, not only letters but also brief notes, written in haste on scraps of paper. Louise Sabati had kept everything, perhaps unbeknown to her lover, almost certainly so, in fact; otherwise she wouldn't have hidden the box under the bed.

"Let me see."

Lomel seemed affected as he read them. He said in a rather unsure voice:

"They're love letters."

The Magistrate noticed at last what was going on.

"Letters?"

"Love letters."

"From whom?"

"From Alain. Signed with his Christian name, sometimes only with his initials."

Maigret, who had read two or three of them, would have liked to stop them being passed around from hand to hand. They were probably the most moving love letters he had ever been privileged to read. The doctor had written them with the ardor and sometimes the naïveté of a young man of twenty.

He called Louise "*My little girl.*"

Sometimes: "*My own poor little girl.*"

And he would tell her, as all lovers do, about the long days and nights without her, the emptiness of his life, the house where, like a hornet, he would bang himself against the walls; he told her he wished he could have known her earlier, before any man had touched her, and of the rages that took hold of him, in the evenings, alone in his bed, when he thought of the caresses she had submitted to.

In certain places, he addressed her like an irresponsible child, and in others he gave way to cries of hate and despair.

"Gentlemen . . ." Maigret began, with a lump in his throat.

They paid no attention to him. It was none of his business. Chabot, blushing, his glasses misty, continued to look through the sheets of paper.

"*I left you half an hour ago and have regained my prison. I need your touch again. . . .*"

He had known her a bare eight months. There were nearly two hundred letters there, and on certain days he had written three, one after the other. Some of them had no stamp. He must have brought them with him.

"If I were a real man . . ."

It was a relief to Maigret when he heard the arrival of the police, moving aside the crowd and the children.

"You'd better take them with you," he whispered to his friend.

They had to be collected from everyone. The men seemed embarrassed as they handed them over. They hesitated now to turn toward the bed, and when they did glance at the outstretched body, it was only furtively, as though to apologize.

As he was now, without his glasses, his face relaxed and serene, Alain Vernoux looked ten years younger than when alive.

"My mother must be getting anxious . . ." Chabot remarked, looking at his watch.

He was forgetting about the house on Rue Rabelais, where there was a whole family, a father, a mother, a wife, children, whom he would have to bring himself to inform.

Maigret reminded him. The Magistrate murmured:

"I would much sooner not go there myself."

The Chief Inspector did not like to offer to do so himself. Perhaps his friend did not like to ask him.

"I shall send Féron."

"Where?" asked the latter.

"To Rue Rabelais, to inform them. Speak to the father first."

"What shall I tell him?"

"The truth."

The little Superintendent muttered under his breath:
"That's a nice job!"

They had nothing more to do here. No more to discover in the room of a poor girl whose sole treasure consisted of a box of letters. Probably she hadn't understood them all. It didn't matter.

"Are you coming, Maigret?"

And, to the doctor:

"Will you take charge of moving the body?"

"To the morgue?"

"A post-mortem will be necessary. I don't see how . . ."

He turned to the two policemen.

"Don't let anyone enter."

He went down the stairs, the cardboard box under his arm, and had to squeeze his way through the crowd gathered below. He hadn't considered the question of a car. They were on the far side of town. Of his own accord, the Bordeaux reporter hurried forward.

"Where would you like me to drive you?"

"To my home."

"On Rue Clemenceau?"

For the most part, they made the journey in silence. Only when they were a hundred yards from his house did Chabot murmur:

"I suppose that's the end of the case."

He couldn't have been too sure, because he examined Maigret out of the corner of his eye. And the latter gave no sign of concurrence, said neither yes nor no.

"I can see no reason, if he wasn't guilty, for . . ."

He stopped short, because, hearing the car, his mother, who must have been consumed with impatience, was already opening the door.

"I was wondering what had happened. I saw people running as though something was going on."

He thanked the reporter, felt he had to offer him something:

"A brandy?"

"No, thanks. I must telephone my paper quickly."

"The joint will be overcooked. I was expecting you at half past twelve. You look tired, Julien. Don't you think, Jules, that he looks pale?"

"You must leave us for a moment, Mama."

"Don't you want to eat?"

"Not right away."

She clutched hold of Maigret.

"Is there anything wrong?"

"Nothing to worry you."

He preferred to tell her the truth, or at least part of the truth.

"Alain Vernoux has committed suicide."

She simply said:

"Ah!"

Then, shaking her head, she went off to the kitchen.

"Let's go into my study. Unless you are hungry?"

"No."

"Help yourself to a drink."

He would have liked a glass of beer, but he knew there was none in the house. He looked in the liqueur cabinet, took out, at random, a bottle of Pernod.

"Rose will bring you water and ice."

Chabot had collapsed into his armchair, where his father's head, before his own, had worn a darker patch in the leather. The shoe box was on the desk, with the ribbon, which had been retied.

The Magistrate urgently needed to be reassured. His nerves were on edge.

"Why don't you take a little brandy?"

From the way Chabot glanced at the door, Maigret realized that it was at his mother's wish that he had given up drinking.

"I prefer not to."

"As you please."

In spite of the mild temperature that day, a fire continued to blaze in the fireplace, and Maigret, who was too hot, had to move away from it.

"What do you think of it?"

"Of what?"

"Of what he's done. Why, if he were not guilty . . ."

"You read some of his letters, didn't you?"

Chabot lowered his head.

"Superintendent Féron invaded Louise's rooms yesterday, questioned her, took her to the police station, kept her all night in a cell."

"He acted without my instructions."

"I know. He did it, all the same. This morning, Alain hurried to see her and learned everything."

"I don't see what difference that made."

He could tell very well, but was refusing to admit it.

"You think it's because of that . . . ?"

"I think that was enough. Tomorrow, the whole town would have known. Féron would probably have gone on badgering the girl; they would finally have condemned her on grounds of prostitution."

"He has been imprudent. But it's not a reason for taking one's own life."

"It depends on who you are."

"You're convinced he is not guilty."

"And you?"

"I think that everyone will believe him guilty and be satisfied."

Maigret looked at him in surprise.

"You mean to say you're going to close the case?"

"I don't know. I just don't know any more."

"Do you remember what Alain told us?"

"What about?"

"That a lunatic has his own logic. A lunatic who's lived all his life without anyone perceiving his madness does not set out all of a sudden to kill without reason. There must be provocation at least. There must be a cause, which may appear insufficient to a person in his senses, but which appears sufficient to him.

"Robert de Courçon was the first victim, and, in my opinion, that's the one that counts, because it's the only one that might provide us with a clue.

"Public opinion doesn't just spring up out of nothing, either."

"You trust the ideas of the masses?"

"It can be mistaken in its demonstrations. However, almost always, I've been able to recognize over the course of the years that there's some serious foundation for it. I would say that the masses have an instinct. . . ."

"So that it really is Alain. . . ."

"I haven't come to that yet. When Robert de Courçon was killed, the townspeople associated the two houses on Rue Rabelais, and, at that time, there was no question of madness. Courçon's murder was not necessarily the deed of a madman or a maniac. It was possible there were precise reasons for someone deciding to kill him, or to do it in a moment of anger."

"Go on."

139

Chabot was giving up the struggle. Maigret could have told him anything, and he would have concurred. He felt that his career, his life, was in the process of being destroyed.

"I know no more than you. There have been two more crimes, one after the other, both inexplicable, both carried out in the same manner, as if the murderer meant to emphasize there was only one and the self-same guilty party."

"I thought that criminals generally kept to one method, always the same."

"I'm wondering, myself, why he was in such a hurry."

"In such a hurry over what?"

"To kill once more. Then to kill yet again. As though to establish fully, in the public mind, that a criminal lunatic was going about the streets."

At this, Chabot raised his head sharply.

"You mean it's not a lunatic?"

"Not exactly."

"Well?"

"It's a question I'm sorry I didn't discuss more thoroughly with Alain Vernoux. The little that he told us about it sticks in my mind. Even a lunatic does not necessarily act like a lunatic."

"That's obvious. Otherwise, there would be none left at large."

"Nor is it, necessarily, because he's a lunatic that he kills."

"I don't follow you any more. What's your conclusion?"

"I've come to no conclusion."

They jumped when they heard the telephone. Chabot lifted the receiver, changed his attitude, his voice.

"But of course, madame. He is here. I'll pass him on to you."

And, to Maigret:

"Your wife."

She was saying at the other end of the line:

"Is that you? I'm not disturbing your lunch? Are you still at the table?"

"No."

It served no purpose to tell her he had not yet eaten.

"Your chief phoned me half an hour ago and asked me if you were definitely returning tomorrow morning. I didn't know what to reply, because when you telephoned me you didn't seem certain. He told me, if I was phoning you again, to inform you that the daughter of some senator or other disappeared two days ago. It's not yet in the newspapers. It seems that it's very important, that there's some risk of a scandal. Do you know who it is?"

"No."

"He gave a name, but I've forgotten it."

"In fact, he wants me to return without fail?"

"He didn't put it quite like that. But I gathered he'd be glad if you'd take charge of the case yourself."

"Is it raining?"

"It's wonderful weather. What are you going to decide?"

"I shall do my utmost to be in Paris by tomorrow morning. There must surely be a night train. I haven't yet looked in the timetable."

Chabot signed to him that there was a night train.

"Is everything going well at Fontenay?"

"Everything's going well."

"Give my regards to the Magistrate."

"I shan't forget."

When he had hung up, he couldn't have told whether his friend was dejected or delighted to find that he was leaving.

"You have to return?"

"It would be best."

"Perhaps it's time we went to luncheon?"

Maigret left the white box, which affected him somewhat as a coffin might, with regret.

"Don't let's mention any of this in front of my mother."

They had not yet reached the dessert when there was a ring at the door. Rose went to open it, came back to announce:

"It's the Superintendent of Police asking for . . ."

"Show him into my study."

"I have done that. He's waiting. He says it's not urgent."

Madame Chabot was making an effort to talk of one thing or another as if nothing were going on. She dug up names from her memory, people who were dead or who had left town a long time ago, whose history she reeled off.

At last they got up from the table.

"Shall I have the coffee brought to your study?"

It was served to all three men, and Rose placed glasses and the bottle of brandy on the tray with an almost ritual gesture. They had to wait for the door to be shut again.

"Well?"

"I went there."

"A cigar?"

"No, thanks. I haven't had lunch yet."

"Would you like me to order something for you?"

"I called my wife to say I wouldn't be long in coming home."

"How did it go?"

"The butler opened the door to me and I asked him if I could see Hubert Vernoux. He left me in the vestibule while he went to inform him. It took a long time. A boy of seven or eight came to look at me from the top of the stairs, and I heard his mother's voice calling him. Someone else observed me through the crack of a door, an old woman, but I don't know if it was Madame Vernoux or her sister."

"What did Vernoux say?"

"He appeared from the end of the hallway and, when he was three or four yards from me, he asked, still coming forward:

" 'Have you found him?'

"I told him I had bad news for him. He didn't invite me into the living room, left me standing on the mat, looking at me from his full height, but I could see clearly that his lips and fingers were trembling.

" 'Your son is dead,' I eventually told him.

"And he replied:

" 'You've killed him?'

" 'He committed suicide, this morning, in his mistress's room.' "

"Did he seem surprised?" asked the Examining Magistrate.

"It seemed to me that it gave him a shock. He looked as though he was about to ask a question, but merely murmured:

" 'So he did have a mistress!'

"He didn't ask me who the mistress was, or what had become of her. He went toward the door to open it,

143

and the last words he spoke, on ushering me out, were:

" 'Now, perhaps, these people will leave us in peace.'

"He jerked his chin toward the onlookers gathered on the sidewalk, the groups standing on the other side of the street, the reporters who were taking advantage of the moment he stood on the doorstep to photograph him."

"He didn't try to avoid them?"

"On the contrary. When he saw them, he paused, facing them squarely, looking them in the eyes, then, slowly, he closed the door, and I heard him fasten the bolts."

"How's the girl?"

"I called in at the hospital. Chabiron is still at her bedside. They aren't sure yet whether she will pull through, because of something wrong with her heart."

Without touching his coffee, he gulped down his glass of brandy, rose to his feet.

"May I go and eat now?"

Chabot nodded and rose in his turn to see him out.

"What shall I do next?"

"I don't know yet. Call in at my office. The Public Prosecutor's meeting me there at three o'clock."

"Just in case, I've left two men outside the house on Rue Rabelais. The crowd's filing by, stopping, arguing in low voices."

"Is it quiet?"

"Now that Alain Vernoux's committed suicide, I don't think there's any more danger. You know how it is."

Chabot looked at Maigret as though to say:

"You see!"

He would have given anything for his friend to have replied:

"Of course. It's all over."

Only, Maigret made no reply.

8

A little before the bridge, as he was coming down from the Chabots' house, Maigret had turned to the right and, for the past ten minutes, he had been following a long road that was neither in the town nor in the country.

To start with, the houses, white, red, gray, including the large residence and storehouses of a wine merchant, were still attached one to another, but it didn't bear the stamp of Rue de la République, for instance, and some of them, whitewashed, without an upper floor, were almost cottages.

Then there had been some gaps, alleyways that allowed glimpses of kitchen gardens descending the slight slope toward the river, once or twice a white goat attached to a stake.

He encountered hardly a soul on the sidewalks, but

through open doors he noticed, in the half-light, families seemingly motionless, listening to the radio or eating pastries, or else a man in his shirt sleeves reading the newspaper, somewhere else again a little old woman dozing beside a grandfather clock with a copper pendulum.

Little by little, the gardens encroached more and more, the gaps between the walls grew wider, the Vendée curved in close to the road, bringing down with it the broken branches from the last squalls.

Maigret, who had refused to let himself be driven by car, was starting to regret it, for he hadn't thought it was such a long way, and the sun was already hot on the back of his neck. He took almost half an hour to reach the Gros-Noyer crossroads, beyond which there seemed to be only meadows.

Three young men dressed in navy blue, their hair oiled, who were leaning against the door of an inn and probably did not know who he was, looked at him with the aggressive irony of peasants for the town-dweller who has strayed among them.

"Madame Page's house?" he asked them.

"You mean Léontine's?"

"I don't know her first name."

That was enough to set them laughing. They found it odd that anyone shouldn't know Léontine's first name.

"If you mean her, try that door over there."

The house they pointed out to him consisted only of a ground floor, so low that Maigret could touch the roof with his hand. The door, painted green, was divided in two, like some stable doors, the upper part being open, the lower closed.

At first, he saw no one in the kitchen, which was very clean, with a white earthenware stove, a round table covered with checked oilcloth, some lilac in a multicolored vase, doubtless won at a fair; the mantelpiece was crowded with knickknacks and photographs.

He pulled a little bell hanging from a piece of string.

"What is it?"

Maigret saw her come out of the bedroom through a door on the left: these were the only rooms in the house. The woman could have been anything from fifty to sixty-five years old. As dry and hard as the chambermaid in the hotel had been, she looked him over with peasantlike mistrust, without coming to the door.

"What do you want?"

Then right away:

"Isn't there a photograph of you in the newspaper?"

Maigret heard someone move in the room. A man's voice inquired:

"Who is it, Léontine?"

"The Chief Inspector from Paris."

"Chief Inspector Maigret?"

"I think that's his name."

"Ask him to come in."

Without moving, she repeated:

"Come in."

He himself lifted the latch to open the lower part of the door. Léontine did not invite him to sit down, said nothing to him.

"You were Robert de Courçon's housekeeper, weren't you?"

"For fifteen years. The police and reporters have already asked me all sorts of questions. I know nothing."

From where he was, the Chief Inspector could now see a white bedroom with the walls adorned with colored prints, the foot of a high walnut bed topped by a red eiderdown, and the smoke of a pipe, which reached his nostrils. The man was still moving about.

"I want to see what he looks like . . ." he was muttering.

And she, to Maigret, in an unfriendly voice:

"Did you hear what my husband said? Go in. He can't leave his bed."

Sitting there, was a man whose face was covered by a beard; newspapers and popular novels were strewn around him. He was smoking a clay pipe with a long stem and, on the bedside table, within reach of his arm, was a liter of white wine and a glass.

"It's his legs," explained Léontine. "Ever since he was jammed between the buffers of two freight cars. He used to work on the railway. It affected his bones."

The lace curtains softened the light and two pots of geraniums brightened the window sill.

"I've read all the stories they tell about you, Monsieur Maigret. I read all day. I never used to read before. Bring a glass, Léontine."

Maigret could not refuse. He clinked glasses. Then, taking advantage of the fact that the wife was still in the room, he brought out of his pocket the piece of lead piping, which he had managed to be allowed to take with him.

"Do you recognize this?"

She did not turn a hair. She said:

"Of course."

"Where did you last see it?"

"On the big living-room table."

"At Robert de Courçon's?"

"At the master's place, yes. It was left over from the repairs, when part of the plumbing had to be changed, last winter, because the frost had burst the water pipes."

"He kept this piece of piping on his table?"

"All sorts of things were there. It was called the living room, but it was the room in which he spent all his time and where he worked."

"You did his housework?"

"As much as he allowed me to do: sweep the floor, dust—but without moving a thing!—and wash the dishes."

"He was a bit crazy."

"I didn't say that."

"You can tell the Chief Inspector," her husband whispered to her.

"I've no complaints to make about him."

"Except there were months when you weren't paid."

"It wasn't his fault. If the others, opposite, had given him the money they owed him . . ."

"You weren't tempted to throw away this pipe?"

"I tried to. He told me to leave it where it was. He used it as a paperweight. I remember he added that it might be useful if burglars tried to break into his house. It was a funny idea, because there were lots of guns on the walls. He collected them."

"Is it true, Chief Inspector, that his nephew's killed himself?"

"It's true."

"Do you think he's the murderer? Have another glass of wine? As far as I'm concerned, as I was telling my wife, I don't try to understand these rich people. They don't think, they don't feel, like us."

"Did you know the Vernouxs?"

"Like anyone else, from meeting them on the street. I've heard it said their money's run out, that they've even borrowed from their servants, and that's probably true since Léontine's boss wasn't getting his allowance any longer and couldn't pay her."

His wife was signaling to him not to talk so much. He hadn't much to say, anyway, but he was glad to have company and to meet Chief Inspector Maigret in the flesh.

The latter left them with a slightly sour taste in his mouth, from the white wine. On his walk back, he found few people about. Some young men and girls on bicycles were returning to the country. A few families were slowly making their way into town.

They were probably still in conference at the Palais, in the Magistrate's office. Maigret had refused to join them, because he did not want to influence the decision they were going to make.

Would they decide to close the inquiry and take the doctor's suicide as an admission of guilt?

It was most likely and, in that case, Chabot would feel a sense of remorse to the end of his life.

When he reached Rue Clemenceau and could see right down the length of Rue de la République, there was quite a crowd; people were walking on both sidewalks, others were coming out of the movies, and, on the terrace of the Café de la Poste, all the chairs were occupied. The sun was already taking on the pinkish hues of sunset.

He made for Place Viète, passed his friend's house, where he caught sight of Madame Chabot behind the second-floor windows. On Rue Rabelais, some inquisitive onlookers were still posted in front of the Vernouxs' house, but, perhaps because there had been a death in the household, people kept at a respectful distance, most of them on the opposite sidewalk.

Maigret repeated to himself once more that this case

was no concern of his, that he had a train to catch that same evening, that he was running the risk of upsetting everyone and falling out with his friend.

After which, incapable of resisting, he reached up his hand to the door knocker. He had to wait a long time, in full view of the passers-by, before he at last heard footsteps and the butler half-opened one side of the door.

"I'd like to see Monsieur Hubert Vernoux."

"Monsieur can't see anyone."

Maigret had entered without being asked. The hall was still in half-darkness. No noise could be heard.

"Is he in his rooms?"

"I think he's lying down."

"One question: do the windows of your room look onto the street?"

The butler seemed uneasy, spoke in a low voice.

"Yes. From the fourth floor. My wife and I sleep in the attics."

"And you can see the house opposite?"

Though they had heard nothing, the living-room door opened, and Maigret recognized the figure of the sister-in-law in the gap.

"What is it, Arsène?"

She had seen the Chief Inspector but did not address him.

"I was telling Monsieur Maigret that Monsieur can't see anyone."

She finally turned to him.

"You would like to speak to my brother-in-law?"

She resigned herself to opening the door wider.

"Come in."

She was alone in the vast living room, with the curtains drawn; one lamp only was alight on a small table. There was no book open, no newspaper, no piece of needlework or anything else. She must have been sitting there, doing nothing, when he had raised the knocker.

"I can receive you instead of him."

"It's he I wish to see."

"Even if you go to his room, he probably won't be in a state to answer your questions."

She walked over to the table where there were a number of bottles, picked up one of them, which had contained Marc de Bourgogne and was now empty.

"It was half full at midday. He wasn't more than a quarter of an hour in this room, while we were still at the table."

"Does this often happen?"

"Practically every day. Now he will sleep until five or six and then he will be glassy-eyed. My sister and I have tried to lock up the bottles, but he finds ways to get around it. It's better it should happen here than in some bar or other."

"Does he go to bars now and again?"

"How can we tell? He goes out by the little door, without our knowing, and then later, when we see his big eyes, when he begins to stammer, it's obvious what it means. He'll end up like his father."

"Has this been going on for a long time?"

"For years. Perhaps he drank before too, and it had less effect on him. He doesn't look his age, but he's sixty-seven, after all."

"I'm going to ask the butler to take me to him."

"Won't you come back later on?"

"I am going back to Paris this evening."

She realized it was useless to argue and pressed a bell. Arsène appeared.

"Take the Chief Inspector to Monsieur."

Arsène looked at her, surprised, as though asking her if she had thought it over.

"We can't help what happens!"

Without the butler, Maigret would have lost himself in the large, echoing hallways intercrossing like those of a convent. He glimpsed a kitchen where copper pots were gleaming and where, as at Le Gros-Noyer, a bottle of white wine was standing on the table, doubtless Arsène's bottle.

The latter seemed not to be able to understand Maigret's attitude any more. Since the question on the subject of his room, he had been expecting a veritable interrogation. Yet he was being asked nothing.

In the right wing of the ground floor he knocked at a carved oak door.

"It's me, Monsieur!" he said, raising his voice so as to be heard inside.

And, when they heard a groan:

"The Chief Inspector is with me and insists on seeing you, Monsieur."

They stood there without moving, while someone walked about the room and eventually opened the door a crack.

The sister-in-law had not been mistaken when she spoke of his big eyes, which fixed on the Chief Inspector in a sort of stupor.

"It's you!" Hubert Vernoux stammered out, in a thick voice.

He must have been lying down completely dressed. His clothes were rumpled, his white hair fell down over his forehead and he passed his hand over it with a mechanical gesture.

"What do you want?"

"I would be glad of an interview with you."

It was difficult to turn away. As though he had not yet recovered his senses, Vernoux drew aside. The room was very large, with a canopied bed of carved wood, very dark, with faded silk draperies.

All the furniture was antique, nearly all of the same style, and made one think of a chapel or a sacristy.

"Will you excuse me a moment?"

Vernoux went through into a bathroom, ran himself a glass of water, and gargled. On returning, he already seemed a little better.

"Sit down. In this armchair if you wish. Have you seen someone?"

"Your sister-in-law."

"She told you I had been drinking?"

"She showed me the bottle of brandy."

He shrugged his shoulders.

"Still the same old story. Women can't understand. A man who's just been brutally informed that his son . . ."

His eyes moistened with tears. The tone of his voice had lowered, almost to a whimper.

"It's a hard blow, Chief Inspector. Especially since he was the only son. What's his mother doing?"

"I've no idea. . . ."

"She will fall ill. It's her little trick. She falls ill and one doesn't dare say anything to her after that. Do you understand? Then, her sister takes her place; she calls it taking charge of the house. . . ."

He reminded one of an old actor trying, at all costs, to stir one's emotions. On his slightly puffy face, the features changed expression at an astonishing rate. In the course of a few minutes, he had successively expressed boredom, a kind of fear, then paternal grief and bitterness with regard to the two women. Now it was fear returning to the surface.

"Why have you insisted on seeing me?"

Maigret, who had not sat down in the armchair indicated to him, took the piece of piping out of his pocket and placed it on the table.

"Did you often visit your brother-in-law?"

"About once a month, to take him his money. I suppose they've heard that I made him a living allowance?"

"Then you've seen this piece of piping on his desk?"

He hesitated, realizing that the reply to this question was of vital importance, and also that he had to make a rapid decision.

"I think I have."

"It's the only material clue they've got in this case. Up to now, they don't seem to have grasped its full significance."

He sat down, took his pipe out of his pocket and filled it. Vernoux remained standing, his features drawn as though he had a violent headache.

"Will you listen to me for a while?"

Without waiting for a reply, he went on:

"It has been asserted that there were three pretty much identical crimes, without it being noticed that the first one was, in fact, completely different from the others. The widow Gibon, like Gobillard too, was killed in cold blood, with premeditation. The man who rang at the former midwife's door went there in order to kill her and did it without waiting in the hall. On the doorstep, he already had his weapon in his hand. When, two days later, he attacked Gobillard, he may not have had him in mind particularly, but he was out of doors in order to kill. Do you understand what I mean?"

Vernoux was, at any rate, making an almost painful effort to guess what Maigret was trying to get at.

"The Courçon case is a different one. On entering his house, the murderer had no weapon. We may deduce from that that he did not come with homicidal intentions. Something occurred which drove him to the deed. Perhaps Courçon's attitude, often provocative, maybe even a threatening move on his part."

Maigret interrupted himself to strike a match and draw on his pipe.

"What do you think of it?"

"Of what?"

"Of my reasoning."

"I thought this case was ended."

"Even supposing it were, I'm trying to understand it."

"A madman would not worry himself over these considerations."

"And if it were not a madman, at any rate not a madman in the usual sense of the word? Listen to me a moment more. Someone calls to see Robert de Courçon, in the evening, without concealing his identity, since he hasn't yet any evil intent, and, for reasons we don't know, is driven to kill him. He leaves no trace behind him, takes the weapon away, which indicates that he doesn't want to be caught.

"It must, therefore, be a man who knows the victim, who's in the habit of going to see him at that time of night.

"The police are bound to search along these lines.

"And there's every chance they'll find the culprit."

Vernoux looked at him with an air of reflection, as though weighing the pros and cons.

"Let us now suppose that another crime is committed, at the other end of town, on someone who has nothing to do with the murderer or with Courçon. What's going to happen?"

The man did not entirely repress a smile. Maigret continued:

"They will not *necessarily* search among the acquaintances of the first victim. The idea that will occur to everybody is that it's a case of madness."

He was silent for a while.

"That is what happened. And the murderer, as an extra safeguard, in order to strengthen the theory of madness, committed a third crime, in the street this time, on the first drunkard he happened to meet. The Examining Magistrate, the Public Prosecutor, the police all fell for it."

"Not you?"

"I wasn't the only one to disbelieve it. Sometimes public opinion is mistaken. Often too it has the same kind of intuition as women and children."

"You mean it pointed to my son?"

"It pointed to this house."

He rose, without pursuing the matter, went toward a Louis XIII table, which served as a desk and on which some writing paper was lying on a blotter. He took one of the sheets, drew a piece of paper from his pocket.

"Arsène wrote," he remarked negligently.

"My butler?"

Vernoux approached quickly, and Maigret noticed that, in spite of his corpulence, he had the lightness of movement that fat men frequently display.

"He wants to be questioned. But he doesn't dare come of his own accord to the police or to the Palais de Justice."

"Arsène knows nothing."

"Maybe, though his room looks onto the street."

"Have you spoken to him?"

"Not yet. I wonder if he bears you a grudge for not paying his wages and for having borrowed money from him."

"You know that too?"

"Have you nothing to tell me yourself, Monsieur Vernoux?"

"What could I tell you? My son . . ."

"Let's not talk about your son. I suppose you've never been happy?"

He did not reply, gazed at the dark floral carpet.

"So long as you had money, the satisfaction of your vanity was enough for you. After all, you were the rich man of the place."

"These are personal questions I don't like discussed."

"Have you lost a lot of money, in the last few years?"

Maigret adopted a lighter tone, as though what he was saying was of no importance.

"Contrary to what you are thinking, the case is not finished and the inquiry remains open. Up to now, for reasons that are no business of mine, the investigations haven't been conducted according to the rules. The interrogation of your servants can't be put off much longer. They will also want to pry into your affairs, examine your bank accounts. They will learn what everybody suspects, that for years now you have been struggling in vain to save the remains of your fortune. Behind the façade there is nothing left, merely a man treated without consideration by his own family, since he's no longer capable of making money."

Hubert Vernoux was about to speak. Maigret did not allow him to begin.

"They will also call in psychiatrists."

He saw his companion raise his head with a sudden jerk.

"I don't know what their opinion will be. I'm not here in any official capacity. I'm returning to Paris this evening, and my friend Chabot still has responsibility for the investigation.

"I told you just now that the first crime was not necessarily the work of a lunatic. I added that the other two were committed for a precise purpose, following a pretty devilish line of reasoning.

"Now, it would not surprise me if the psychiatrists regarded that line of reasoning as an indication of madness, a particular kind of madness more common than one might think, which they call paranoia.

"Have you read the books your son must have in his study?"

"I've sometimes looked through them."

"You should reread them."

"You're not suggesting that I . . ."

"I am suggesting nothing. I saw you yesterday playing cards. I saw you win. You're probably convinced you will win this game in the same way."

"I am not playing any game."

He protested weakly, flattered, really, that Maigret paid so much attention to him, rendering an indirect homage to his astuteness.

"I just want to put you on your guard against committing one error. It wouldn't help matters, quite the reverse, if there were to be more killings, or even a single crime. Do you understand what I mean? As your son emphasized, madness has its own rules, its own logic."

Once more Vernoux was about to speak and still the Chief Inspector would not let him do so.

"I have finished. I'm catching the nine-thirty train and I must go and pack my suitcase before dinner."

His companion, dismayed, disappointed, was looking at him as if completely lost, made a movement as though to detain him, but the Chief Inspector was moving to the door.

"I shall find my own way."

It took him some time, but then he found the kitchen, out of which Arsène sprang, with a questioning look.

Maigret said nothing to him, followed the central hallway, himself opened the front door, which the butler closed behind him.

There were no more than three or four persistently curious people left on the sidewalk opposite. Would the watch committee, this evening, continue its patrols?

He very nearly went to the Palais de Justice, where the meeting was doubtless still continuing, but decided he would do what he had said he would and went to pack his suitcase. After which, in the street, he felt he wanted a glass of beer and sat down on the terrace of the Café de la Poste.

Everyone was looking at him. They talked in lower tones. Some of them started to whisper.

He drank two big glasses, slowly, savoring them, as if he were on a terrace on the Grands Boulevards, and parents were stopping to point him out to their children.

He saw Chalus, the schoolmaster, go past, in company with a potbellied gentleman, to whom he was relating a story, gesticulating all the while. Chalus didn't notice the Chief Inspector and the two men disappeared around the corner.

It was almost dark and the terrace had become empty when he got painfully to his feet to make his way to Chabot's house. The latter came to open the door for him and cast him a troubled glance.

"I was wondering where you were."

"On a café terrace."

He hung his hat on the stand in the hall, saw the table laid in the dining room, but dinner wasn't ready and his friend ushered him first into his study.

After quite a long silence, Chabot muttered without looking at Maigret:

"The inquiry continues."

He seemed to be saying:

"You've won. You see! We aren't so feeble after all."

Maigret did not smile, made a little sign of approval.

"From now on, the house on Rue Rabelais is being guarded. Tomorrow, I will get on with interrogating the servants."

"By the way, I was almost forgetting to return this to you."

"Are you really going this evening?"

"I must."

"I wonder if we shall arrive at an answer."

The Chief Inspector had laid the lead piping on the table, was searching his pockets for Arsène's letter.

"How's Louise Sabati?" he inquired.

"She seems to be out of danger. Her vomiting saved her life. She had just eaten and hadn't begun to digest."

"What has she said?"

"She answers only in monosyllables."

"She knew they were both going to die?"

"Yes."

"Was she resigned to it?"

"He told her that they would never leave them happily alone."

"He didn't talk to her about the three crimes?"

"No."

"Nor about his father?"

Chabot looked him in the eyes.

"Do you think he's the man?"

Maigret merely blinked his eyes.

"Is he mad?"

"The psychiatrists will decide."

"In your opinion?"

"I'm glad to say again that people in their senses do not commit murder. But it's only an opinion."

"Perhaps not very orthodox?"

"No."

"You seem uneasy."

"I'm waiting."

"For what?"

"For something to happen."

"You think something will happen today?"

"I hope so."

"Why?"

"Because I paid a visit to Hubert Vernoux."

"You told him . . ."

"I told him how and why the three crimes were committed. I let him know how the murderer would normally react."

Chabot, so proud a moment ago of the decision he had taken, appeared frightened again.

"But . . . in that case . . . aren't you afraid that . . ."

"Dinner is served," Rose came in to announce, while Madame Chabot, on her way to the dining room, smiled at them.

9

Once again, because of the old lady, they had to be quiet, or, rather, to speak only of this and that, without any bearing on what was on their minds, and, that evening, the topic was cooking, in particular the method of dressing hare *à la royale.*

Madame Chabot had made profiteroles again and Maigret ate five of them, feeling slightly sick, his eyes ceaselessly fixed on the hands of the old clock.

At half past eight, nothing had yet happened.

"You needn't hurry. I've ordered a taxi to go to your hotel first and pick up your luggage."

"Still, I must go there to pay my bill."

"I telephoned to say they were to charge it to me. That'll teach you not to stay with us when, once in a whole twenty years, you deign to come to Fontenay...."

Coffee was served, and brandy. He accepted a cigar, because it was the tradition, and his friend's mother would have been upset if he had refused.

It was five minutes to nine and the car was purring at the door, the driver was waiting, when the telephone bell rang at last.

Chabot hurried over, lifted the receiver.

"Speaking, yes . . . How? . . . Is he dead? . . . I can't hear you, Féron. . . . Don't speak so loud. . . . Yes . . . I'll come immediately. . . . See that he's taken to the hospital; I don't need to tell you. . . ."

He turned to Maigret.

"I must go up there right away. Is it vital that you return tonight?"

"Without fail."

"I won't be able to accompany you to the station."

Because of his mother, he said no more, seized his hat, his light coat.

Only when they were on the sidewalk did he murmur:

"There's been a dreadful scene at the Vernoux's. Hubert Vernoux, dead drunk, started smashing up everything in his room, and finally, in a frenzy, gashed his wrist with his razor."

The Chief Inspector's composure astonished him.

"He isn't dead," Chabot continued.

"I know."

"How do you know?"

"Because men like him don't commit suicide."

"Yet his son . . ."

"You go. They're waiting for you."

The station was only five minutes away. Maigret went over to the taxi.

"We've just enough time," said the driver.

The Chief Inspector turned one last time to his friend, who seemed lost in the middle of the sidewalk.

"Write to me."

It was a monotonous journey. At two or three stations, Maigret got off to have a glass of brandy, and finally dozed off, vaguely conscious, at each stop, of the station-master's shouts and the creaking of the baggage and food carts.

He arrived in Paris in the early morning and a taxi drove him home, where from below he smiled up at the open window. His wife was waiting for him on the landing.

"Not too tired? Did you sleep a little?"

He drank three large cups of coffee before relaxing.

"Are you going to have a bath?"

Certainly he was going to have one! It was good to find Madame Maigret's voice again, the smell of the flat, the furniture and objects in their places.

"I didn't quite understand what you said to me on the telephone. Were you involved in a case?"

"It's over."

"What was it?"

"A fellow who couldn't face losing."

"I don't understand."

"It doesn't matter. There are people who are capable of anything rather than tumble down the slope."

"You must know what you're talking about," she murmured philosophically, without bothering more about it.

At half past nine, in the Commissioner's study, they gave him the known facts about the disappearance of the senator's daughter. It was a sordid story, with almost orgiastic meetings in a cellar and drug-taking as the main item.

"It's pretty certain that she didn't leave of her own free will and it's unlikely she was kidnapped. Most probably she's died from too strong a dose of drugs and her friends, in panic, have got rid of her body."

Maigret copied a list of names, addresses.

"Lucas has already heard some of them. Up to now no one's been prepared to talk."

Wasn't it his job to make people talk?

"Did you enjoy yourself?"

"Where?"

"In Bordeaux."

"It rained the whole time."

He did not mention Fontenay. He hardly had time to think about it for three days, which he spent hearing the confessions of young idiots who thought themselves smart.

Then, in his mail, he found a letter with the postmark of Fontenay-le-Comte. From the newspapers, he already knew, roughly, the epilogue to the case.

Chabot, in his neat, regular writing, rather sharply pointed, which might have been taken for a woman's hand, furnished him with the details.

"At some point, shortly after your departure from Rue Rabelais, he stole down to the cellar and Arsène saw him come back up with a bottle of Napoleon brandy that had been in the Courçon family for two generations."

Maigret could not help smiling. Hubert Vernoux, for his last drunken bout, had not been content with any old spirits. He had chosen the rarest in the house, a venerable bottle they had preserved partly as a proof of nobility.

167

"When the butler came to tell him that dinner was served, his eyes were already haggard, red-rimmed. With a great theatrical gesture, he ordered him to leave him alone, shouted at him:

" 'Let the bitches dine without me!'

"The women sat down at the table. About ten minutes later, heavy thumps were heard coming from his rooms. Arsène was sent to see what was happening, but the door was locked, and Vernoux was meantime smashing up all he could lay hands on and shrieking obscenities.

"When they told her what was happening, it was his sister-in-law who suggested:

" 'The window . . .'

"They did not disturb themselves, remained sitting in the dining room while Arsène went out into the yard. One window was half open. He drew the curtains apart. Vernoux saw him. He already had a razor in his hand.

"He yelled again to leave him alone, that he had had enough, and, according to Arsène, continued to utter filthy words nobody had ever heard him use before.

"While the butler was calling for help, because he did not dare enter the room, the man began to slash his wrist. The blood spurted out. Vernoux looked at it in terror, and thereupon stopped what he was doing. A few seconds later, he fell quite limp on the carpet, unconscious.

"Ever since, he refuses to answer any questions. At the hospital, the next day, they found him ripping up his mattress and they had to lock him in a padded cell.

"Desprez, the psychiatrist, came from Niort to give him a first examination; tomorrow he will have a consultation with a specialist from Poitiers.

"According to Desprez, there is scarcely any doubt of

Vernoux's madness, but, because of the publicity the case is receiving in the district, he nonetheless prefers to take every precaution.

"I have given permission for Alain's burial. The funeral takes place tomorrow. The Sabati girl is still in the hospital and is doing very well. I don't know what to do about her. Her father must be working somewhere in France, but we can't get hold of him. I can't send her back to her rooms, since she still has ideas of suicide.

"My mother talks of taking her as a maid in the house so that she can give a little help to Rose, who is getting old. I'm afraid that people . . ."

Maigret did not have time to finish reading the letter that morning, because they were bringing him an important witness. He stuffed it in his pocket. What became of it, he never knew.

"By the way," he announced that evening to his wife, "I had a letter from Julien Chabot."

"What does he say?"

He searched for the letter, could not find it. It must have fallen out of his pocket when he was pulling out his handkerchief or his tobacco pouch.

"They are going to take on a new maid."

"Is that all?"

"Practically."

It was a long time after, while looking at himself anxiously in the mirror, that he muttered:

"I found that he had aged."

"Who are you talking about?"

"Chabot."

"How old is he?"

"Within two months of me."

Madame Maigret was tidying the room, as she always did before going to bed.

"He should have got married," she concluded.

Shadow Rock Farm
Lakeville, Connecticut
27th March 1953